God's

Hangman

A Monument of Grace

A Novella

R H Brassington

Published by R H Brassington & Printed by CreateSpace 2018.

CreateSpace, Independent Publishing Platform, Charleston, South Carolina.

ISBN-13: 978-1727795424
ISBN-10: 1727795423

CONTENTS

PROLOGUE

Four prison walls, thickened with fear, hurt and hate surround us. We're incarcerated by our past, our low-road choices in our high-minded pride. We've been found guilty. We sit on the floor of a dusty cell awaiting our final moment. Our executioner's footsteps echo against the stone walls. Head between knees, we don't look up as he opens the door; we don't open our eyes as he begins to speak. We know what he's going to say; "Time to pay for your sins." But then you hear something else: "You're free to go. They took Jesus instead of you."

The door swings open, the guard barks: "Get out!" and we find ourselves in the light of the morning sun, shackles gone, crimes pardoned, wondering, "What just happened?"

Grace happened! Christ took away your sins.

WFTD Tues 15th May 2018   Bob and Debby Gass. UCB publications.

4

CHAPTER 1

ON HER MAJESTY'S SERVICE 1885

I don't know which was worse: the cold hollow sound of the prison bell or the sharp sound of approaching footsteps on stone flags, but both seemed to create an eerie harmony as they echoed along the walls and corridors of the time-soaked Exeter building. Either way, both sent a penetrating shudder to one's very soul. Outside, the cold morning February bite was no less benevolent than the prison's ancient thick, grey walls which so many times in the past had concealed the horrors which can only be described as man's inhumanity to his fellow man. A short straight corridor with directed foot-worn stone paving led from the condemned cell, a last peaceful abode, to what might be described in those days as a new humane way of dispatching the damned to eternity. It was none other than the "Long Drop" method of hanging, pioneered by William Marwood, and presumably intended to be swift, clean and maybe even painless. It was this fate that John "Babbacombe" Lee pensively awaited.

Exeter's prison gallows was nothing more than a converted makeshift, in what was at other times used as a coach house where carriages were stored and kept in peak condition by one caring mechanic. Raife, a spindly, sharp-featured little man who had a voice almost as harsh as his name sounded, was the sole artisan and maintainer of both contraptions of passage. It seemed weird that both his job briefs were concerned with travel of one kind or another; one designed for earthly destinations, the other eternal. But this was his job, his trade, and come what may, he had little time for trivialities, and this attitude certainly earned him some kind of respect. When times were slack at Exeter he would occasionally be called upon to lend his expertise at some other prison where an execution was pending. Checking the crude mechanism of these deadly contraptions was of course his forte, and wasn't something that anyone really wanted to get involved with. On the other hand his skills were sometimes watched by others with what can only be described as a weird if not somewhat unhealthy fascination. Either way the authorities of the various prisons he visited welcomed, if only through necessity, his artisan prowess.

This greasy, little, Cornish country bumpkin turned gallows inspector had been meticulously working on the Exeter scaffold the day prior to Lee's execution. Because it had rained heavily during the night, and given that the coach house roof left much to be desired, most of the timbers and iron mechanisms associated with the "contraption" were now in need of urgent attention. The wooden planking was beginning to swell, so immediate action had to be taken to ensure quick and efficient opening of the trap.

"Err everything alright for tomorrow Mr Raife?" chirped an anxious voice from the corner of the yard.

"Arr," replied Raif in his usual broad tone. "Soon 'ave this lot sorted. Bid o' damp aint gonna stop ol' Raify's lady doin' 'er bit, can't disappoint the crowd nouw can we? … Hee hee. Drop o' oil an an a touch o' the ol' wood plane 'll soon 'ave 'er as good as noo. The show must go on yer know Mr Berry."

James Berry was no ordinary hangman. Having apprenticed his craft under the auspices of William Marwood, Berry was one of a new breed of hangmen who took his trade seriously. He was a well-built, dark haired Yorkshire man with heavy features who had begun his career as a policeman. He had a deep scar extending down his cheek from the corner of his right eye partly obscured by a neat beard. Across his forehead was another great scar, the result of a scuffle whilst arresting a violent character in a public house. He was always smartly dressed even down to the gold watch & chain with which he occasionally fiddled, as if to remind himself of the importance of the punctuality his profession required. Arriving 2nd class by train from his home in Bradford, Berry had come straight from the station to the prison before being shown to the "guest room" – his "hotel" for the duration – which wasn't much better than a cell with a few added comforts. His first job was to make himself familiar with the vital equipment after first engaging in a short prayer, as Berry was indeed a pious man who felt his ministry of retribution was also a righteous calling. Yet in spite of his legalistic hardness, and even being regarded by some people as a monster, Berry could show a tender heart and a genuine concern for the condemned. He had even been known to forward poems and prayers that he'd copied from journals – hoping it might help them face their ordeal.

"Show?" retorted Berry. "Show must go on! This is not a circus as you so flippantly put it! This is the administration of justice as English Law requires. And mark this, when the culprit is *hanged by the neck until dead* tomorrow morning he'll 'ave paid his debt to society and we judge him n' longer – the rest's up to the Almighty!"

"Arr well 'suppose your roight an all thaat Mr Berry, don' wanna to corze any offence do we nouw, 'ts just thaat this jarb sometimes gets a bid morbid y' see – just lightenin' things up a bid yer know."

Berry turned away as if he hadn't heard and looked towards the contraption which was more important.

Stepping up onto the raised rampart Berry gave what appeared to be a short forgiving nod towards Raife, then purposed to give close inspection to the heavy iron shackle and supporting oak beam which would anchor the fateful rope.

"Hmm … aye Mr Raif that looks solid enough t' me, what about the operation, can I have a feel at that theer lever o'er there?"

"Ye can thaat Mr Berry."

Raife took a rag to wipe off a few oily smears from the iron handle of the large lever and politely stepped aside for the "master's" inspection.

"Wouldna wanner do yar jarb Mr Berry … does it ever get to ye an all?"

"Aye lad sometimes it does, but 'suppose somebody's gotta do it."

"D' ye think any of 'em get t' 'eaven when they've paid as ye say, or are they all doomed to 'ell when they fall down thaat 'ole there?"

Berry had to smile somewhat at the Cornishman whose simplicity of thought seemed quite profound.

Suddenly Berry's mood changed as if by some seizure or sudden realisation of something – he was focussed in thought – he'd forgotten something. Raife looked startled and momentarily shuddered as he caught the hard dark expression in the hangman's eyes. Without saying a word Berry smartly walked off the platform and strode across the yard and disappeared through the security door at the far end. Such mood swings were not uncommon for this extraordinary man whose job dictated his demeanour. Raife shrugged his shoulders and carried on sweeping up a few shavings, picking up the odd nail, bolt etc. and generally making the place look clean and tidy as Berry had ordered.

Unknown to Raife, Berry had forgotten the most important component for the task at hand – the rope! Without this of course the execution could not happen. The rope was purpose made and was the sole piece or tool which Berry always took with him on his missions. Skilfully made to his requirements with brass eye, plus the chamois leather sleeve in order to avoid marking the skin on the culprit's neck, Berry's rope was designed to adjust to the set length according to the "Book of Drops" he had so meticulously tabulated.

Raife scurried around completing a few more menial tasks then decided *all was well* and nimbly picking up his oily tool bag, spritely followed the same route as Berry to the main security gate, and the outside world.

Back in his guest room, the now becalmed Berry was un-strapping what appeared to be a brown soft leather carrying bag. Reverently putting his hand inside he respectfully lifted out a white cotton sack with a hemmed cord, followed by a stout length of hemp rope. Using two hands he held the piece at some distance from his body and pondered.

"Dear Lord", he murmured. "Why do I do this awful job? I wish I didn't have to do this tomorrow."

When the awful day came, Berry would rise early enough to begin with a short prayer. Inner struggles like this were common. In his head he saw the need for capital punishment as atonement, but his soul struggled with the fact that he was taking a human life, and this meant he was no better than the murderer.

Back in the condemned cell, for Lee, time was now up. With the sound of those approaching footsteps Lee's heartbeat was quickened; in a short time from now it would all be over; yet his mind raced with the turmoil of events leading to the day he was captured by a hunting mob – the beginning of the end of freedom. He gazed at the sky through a high barred window, in entranced focus on a small patch of blue yonder in what was otherwise a murky grey February day, and suddenly everything about life seemed so precious.

CHAPTER 2

THE CHASE

Poor Lee. How time was ebbing away. How he felt robbed. How he wished he could put the clock back. How he wished he could swap his short time left for just one more yesterday – even if it was the day of that awful chase on Dartmoor.

It was as if the whole county had turned out that November day on Dartmoor when Lee was finally caught. In vengeful chase and determined ferocity, hounds, horses, farm folk and all seemed to revert to a medieval hue and cry, in frenzied pursuit of the wretched youth.

Suddenly the shriek of a huntsman's horn commanded everyone's attention.

"There he is!" bellowed a mounted scout who had been high positioned on the moor.

"C'mon folks … We've spotted him – we'll have him by tonight," cried one of the group leaders in response.

That gave the mob momentum, and like a pack of possessed jackals hungry for the kill they closed in on him.

Lee to them was nothing more than an animal now – a target; he had done wrong and was going to get what he deserved no matter what!

Poor misunderstood Lee. Had it not been for fate of circumstance just a few days ago, this day would not have existed.

 "Why oh God – why me? Why should this be my fate now just when things were looking brighter? God only knows I didn't do it!   How could I end such a beautiful life like hers? I know Lord I've been a scoundrel and deserve nothing – nothing! I know I've stolen and cheated and been bad oh so bad … but I would never kill anyone, and I would never hurt Miss Keyes!"

Bedraggled and shivering due to a combination of fear and cold, Lee was hiding in what was probably the sodden hollow of a collapsed mine entrance, well concealed on boggy Dartmoor, hoping that nightfall would come before the mob captured him. His mind racing with the horror of it all, he'd managed to make good distance for most of the day and would have almost got far enough from his pursuers to be able to lie low for a while and gather himself and then think about what he might do next. But common sense told him that trying to make headway over Dartmoor in November was not only difficult but dangerous. The hazards were enormous: from a high risk of sinking into one of the treacherous bogs, made worse by winter snow and rain, to exposure from freezing fog that could bring on hypothermia within a very short space of time, particularly for someone who was not prepared. But Lee thought it was worth a try hoping they wouldn't search for him in such bleak conditions.

Maybe this'll work, Lee had thought to himself. *Maybe they'll think if I'm mad enough to try to cross the moor in these conditions I'll die anyway and then they'll give up the chase.*

With this desperate thought in mind he knew of only one possible hideout – an old tin mine on the far edge of the moor. If only he could get to that he would be far enough away from his pursuers and could shelter from the harsh winter bite.

But what seemed like a good idea at the time to Lee was a plan that the local chasers had suspected. Such desperate plans by criminals escaping on moors in this area were well known by the police and prison authorities. Many a criminal and prison escapee had often been chased across moors such as Dartmoor and the Authorities knew only too well that in most cases the old tin mines were an obvious destination to *hole up* for a while. But they were still a fair bet for someone on the run, as some of the old mines were so dangerous due to neglect that only a fool would risk delving deep into the precarious bowels of some of their gaseous and flooded caverns, which hopefully meant that their pursuers would not dare take the risk themselves. Of course there were stories told of those who did take such desperate measures to hide from capture only to remain entombed, which would be looked upon as poetic justice and of course would save the Authorities any further expense.

But any hope of this for Lee was not to happen. It had been increasingly difficult to maintain a fast pace over the craggy landscape of the upper moor; his heavily-slowing limbs and weakening ankles were strongly signalling the need to rest. Suddenly without warning he felt a sickening "crack!" He had gone over on his ankle and was losing balance. Totally exhausted now and stumbling out of control, he felt his fatigued body hurl itself downwards into the miry hollow of the collapsed mine entrance – ending with a dark depressing thud.

For a while Lee couldn't move – neither did he want to or even care.

Best to stay here now and take what fate has to offer – perhaps just die, he thought to himself.

And so here he was – murmuring to himself with a head spinning and full of questions.

"But it didn't work God … what were you doing? Where were you? And where are you now I ask? Me, trying to be good didn't work."

"Miss Keyes was my friend, the only person who understood … beautiful Christian lady. The only one in this cruel world to give me a chance – second chance, and more, her kindness won me over. Life for once had meaning, purpose. For once in my life I was beginning to understand what dignity and self-respect was all about."

"Even the plumber, who came to mend Miss Keyes' burst pipe, gave me hope — real hope. I never heard anything like it. He said Jesus could be my best friend if I really wanted to change and was willing to give Him a chance, he called it grace or something. Please Mr God, Mr Grace or whatever I'm supposed to call you – save me! Get me out of this mess – you're just about my only hope now!"

As Lee sobbed himself into a hunched pathetic ball in the muddy ditch, enveloped in his own self-pity he was unaware of the constable quietly easing himself down the sludgy embankment to stealthily creep up on him from behind, finally resting a firm yet compassionate hand on his shoulder.

"C'mon lad – c'mon now." A deep solemn voice called him out of his daydream.

If Lee had ever awakened from one nightmare to another then this was surely it!

What had been a deep reminiscent daydream reliving the chase on Dartmoor had come crashing into the cold reality of his now presence in the condemned cell. And what he had dreamt to be the voice of an apprehending constable on Dartmoor was really a prison officer informing Lee that it was "time!"

"C'mon … hey… c'mon lad now … it's time," continued the Officer's firm command.

Startled into realization by a sudden pinioning of his hands behind his back Lee became aware of the speed at which the next process was approaching.

And it hit him with full force.

CHAPTER 3

DEAD MAN WALKING

"**N**o! God! No, no!"

An immediate struggle ensued – nothing new to the prison entourage, in fact it was partly expected, but easily contained by a couple of hefty prison guards and a fat priest.

"The truth! ... the whole... t' ruth and nothing b'but the ... truth ... they said at the trial. I told them the truth! I... I – trusted them! So why didn't they believe me?"

His heartfelt cry to be heard – his plea; punctuated by contorted twists of resistance against the guards simply landed on deaf ears. With hoarse incoherence, Lee spluttered out his feeble fragment of hope – but there was no hope. Finally breaking into a yielding gasp, Lee now hung bent forward under the support of the two prison officers.

Correcting any untidiness in their black tunics and uniforms with an odd brush or tug of hand, the legal assembly smartly repositioned themselves into correct order.

"I am the Resurrection and the life sayeth the Lord …" The priest was very skilful at this point.

Redirecting focus away from the momentary eventful seizure, he moaned out the traditional burial service, as was usual in these cases, quickly leading out the procession into the musty corridor. Recovering any lost dignity, the entourage made their way along the flaky whitewashed corridor in correct, orderly fashion as stipulated by prison policy. The procession was led first by the priest, then came the prison governor, the undersheriff, two guards either side of the prisoner, a surgeon and last but not least the hangman. Because of Lee's temporary loss of strength as a result of his heavy physical resistance the two guards almost carried him – feet dragging the first few steps until the succumbed wretch managed to keep his own pace.

"… he who believes in me shall not die but have everlasting life sayeth the Lord," continued the hollow moan of the priest leading the way and peering with spectacled glances over his well-thumbed prayer book.

Shall not die … shall not die …what does that mean? Lee thought to himself.

Could it be ... could it be ...? Yes the plumber... yes ... he said that.

Within the psychotic whirl of confusion it was if Lee's very soul was trying to tear itself from his mortal frame. His numb, lifeless body seemed to be giving up its ghost as if in premature anticipation of what was to come – an act of grace? *Is the Almighty going to spare me the final act and take me now?* he thought. He had never experienced anything like this. Whether it was due to some desperate urge to break free from captivity or just sheer exhaustion one couldn't be sure. But this powerfully surging inner will shook his very core. Like a drowning man desperate for air, he felt himself break free from his robotic body with a loud inner "pop!" suddenly finding himself at a remote elevated position near the ceiling of the corridor and feeling freer than he had ever felt before.

Perhaps this is it, he thought to himself. *Perhaps I'm dead.*

Lee was now looking down on what seemed to be his own body walking amidst the procession. In a unique way he had been allowed to see his mortal frame as if from some remote camera. Hardly recognising his own pathetic form he felt he should have been horrified by it all – but no! The tranquillity of this "out of body experience" had somehow shielded him from any fear – he was free!

Next he found himself transported, as if in some kind of astral dreamlike state through time and space, yet very much alert. He saw Miss Keyes' cottage – he was there. The plumber was there, and so was Miss Keyes. Oh dear Miss Keyes how he longed to hear her warm comforting voice. The whole transcendent experience was becoming a re-enactment of past events. The two of them spoke about wonderful yet strange things that Lee had never heard of before. He had been intrigued by the plumber; this amazing man who seemed to inspire such faith and transmit so much love yet with a boldness which gave you a feeling of self-worth and that nothing else mattered in the world except the message he carried. He'd been to Miss Keyes' house a couple of times to repair burst pipes due to the early seasonal frost which had taken many by surprise sooner than expected. Although it wasn't his main job now, as he was only visiting the area which involved "lots of meetings" or something so he said, he'd offered to help Miss Keyes out due to his previously being trained as a plumber. Miss Keyes had somehow had some kind of connection with the meetings and had gained much help and encouragement from them. He was quite a charismatic character and one couldn't help feeling good in his presence. He was light hearted, often funny but graciously sincere when he needed to be. Lee often found himself secretly smiling at his northern Yorkshire accent which somehow added further humour when he was telling his stories.

The plumber hardly ever seemed to sound his H's and if ever he did he usually put them in the wrong places. This used to make both Lee and Miss Keyes chuckle when he'd left. But he was a great man who would hold no punches when it came to talking about his faith. It was through this man that Lee had heard the gospel for the first time in his life. The plumber spoke about Jesus as if he knew him personally, as if he was in the next room or something. Either way Lee always came away from his nonchalant chats and earwigging between the plumber and Miss Keyes, feeling better for it.

As a young failed seafarer this lad had had nothing but scrapes and brushes with the law, even doing a spell in jail for theft – much exacerbated by bad company – at least that was until Miss Keyes had sought to take him under her wing for a while. Being the good Christian soul that she was, she often felt it her moral duty towards anyone who might be downtrodden and could benefit from a helping hand to get them back into restoring their respectability. Lee of course was a prize candidate in her eyes. She found him some small gardening duties around her place, admittedly for only a small wage, but which she hoped would at least give him the benefit of self-worth.

He had responded admirably to her benevolence and could see a ray of hope and the means to get back some integrity. Adding some thrust to this of course was his odd encounter with the plumber.

The events leading to that fateful day were crystal clear now to John Lee as if watching the whole thing as a play. He saw himself. He saw the Grange with its sloping gardens leading down to the beach. Two people were walking very close to each other; a woman and a man. He looked closer and immediately he recognised the woman; it was Elizabeth his half-sister; they were arguing, she seemed distressed, pleading with the man for some kind of understanding, but his response was cold and negative. Who was he? John tried to focus through the vision's haze but it was as if a dark cloud was enveloping the man – hiding him from view and preventing anyone from knowing who he was. Suddenly the scene changed. He was now in the cottage; it was candle lit creating eerie shadows and concealing a macabre presence. Miss Keyes appeared next wearing a flowing nightgown, long shoulder-length hair and with an anxious look on her face. She gingerly walked down the stairs, her expression becoming more and more fearful as she slowly realised that she had been disturbed by an intruder. She was holding a lantern at head height as if looking for something or someone; then she swiftly turned as if shocked by surprise to encounter the full force of a brutal blow from an axe as the dark figure of her assailant bludgeoned her onto the stone flags of the kitchen floor. What horror! Lee was mortified by the sight. *Who was this demon?* he thought to himself. Gradually the hideous phantom turned towards Lee as if it knew he was watching. At first the face seemed obscured and distorted but then ... horror! Lee was staring at the very face of the person he feared to see the most – himself! It was his face, as if staring at a looking glass. He recoiled in shock – he, a blood stained ruthless killer, who had brought such a terrible end to the life of Miss Anna Keyes; finally trying to destroy all evidence of foul play by pouring lamp oil over her frail body, and engulfing the whole scene in flames.

Of course John Lee knew he was innocent of this dastardly crime. He knew the illusion he saw only illustrated what had been fabricated and envisioned by those who had cobbled together circumstantial evidence against him based only on the hearsay of his sister – his flesh and blood! Her testimony that he was the only one in the house at the time fitted well with the fact that having blood on his arm pointed to guilt, even though it was an obvious possibility that he had cut his arm breaking in to the blazing room in a desperate attempt to rescue Miss Keyes.

Suddenly John was back looking over the beach again but this time Elizabeth was alone she was looking up at him – *Where was the stranger?* he wondered. *Who was he?*

Elizabeth was looking hard at him now as if trying to tell him something. She seemed so sad and tearful – with an apologetic demeanour as if trying to tell him how sorry she'd been for not standing by him at the trial and having to trust in Miss Keyes' lawyer – Templeton, to fight his defence.

Of course! he thought. *It all suddenly fits together. Templeton was Miss Keyes' lawyer and Templeton looked after Miss Keyes affairs ... A beneficiary?... And ... and ... Templeton was the mystery man I saw on the beach with Elizabeth! And Templeton deceived me into trusting him to fight my defence only to leave me high and dry at the last minute by claiming he was ill or something – damn him! ... And Templeton was the killer! Of course ... it's clear now – it was all a plot to set me up making me believe all I had to do was keep quiet, leave it up to him and he would get me off, and then pull out at the last minute leaving me at the mercy of a bumbling incompetent lawyer who would have no time to prepare the case ... how clever!*

The whole mystical experience had probably lasted for only a few seconds yet to John Lee it had been timeless. But it was now beginning to ebb away and John was finding himself being drawn back into his body as if falling backwards and watching the "visions" he had just perceived disappear as if through the wrong end of a telescope. And then he was back; back inside his feeble frame, and back amongst the

26

procession which by now had left the main prison building and was making its way across the courtyard towards the scaffold.

Despite a dreary overcast start to the morning the sunlight had managed to break through by now with an unusual dazzle, which had the timely effect of raising ones spirits, and also put emphasis on the precious gift of life. Two of the leading officials paused for a moment to shield their eyes from the momentary glare which consequently distracted the rest of the procession including the condemned man. Shocked into realising the full implications of events and the reality of what was to follow, Lee froze to the spot. Heels digging in with stiffened body and mortified horror he refused to go any further.

"Stop! Stop! Stop!" he cried.

"It's Templeton! It's him! He did it! … I saw him."

With that, the procession was forced to come to a halt whilst re-grouping and jostling to contain the momentary disruption of proceedings.

"I've seen it all ... seen it in a ... in a ...vision ... I know the truth now, you're hanging the ... the wrong man!" he went on.

"Alright lad ... alright ..." calmly uttered a controlling voice.

"N'no! It's right… the truth ... Miss Keyes ... she knows ... look … look she's there – ask her!"

Convincingly he tried to indicate the direction of her presence with a twist of shoulder and nod of head, wrenching hard on the straps binding his wrists; only to receive sceptical glances of disbelief from his captors.

Lee was truly in a state of euphoric shock, staring at the sudden appearance of another member of the procession. A transfigured apparition of what he believed to be Miss Keyes was directly in front of him only a few feet away. She stood, half turned –her head slightly cocked towards him and immersed in a smiling sunlit aura.

"Aye … aye, alright then, so yer say, but she's not gonna save yer ... you'll be seein' her soon enough ... it's too late now for any o' that … it's no good, yer know you've been found guilty, there's gonna be no reprieve."

"Arr … best face what yr deserve lad," piped up another member of the group.

"C'mon let's get him up there quick now, sounds like he's having delusions or something ... let's get it over with ... sooner the better," muttered the governor.

But the supernatural manifestation was not without result. John Lee appeared to quickly assume a relaxed demeanour as if the personal apparition of "Miss Keyes" had infused a state of inner peace, and Divine assurance that what was about to take place would not happen.

CHAPTER 4

ONLY BELIEVE

If Lee had gained any faith or Divine assurance in his being saved from the gallows it was about to be put to the test. He had been swiftly moved and placed in position standing over the trap which would soon release him into eternity. The procession had ascended the scaffold rampart and each member had assumed their pre-arranged positions with professional efficiency in order to carry out their solemn legal duties. Speed of operation was the rule now so as not to prolong any more suffering for the condemned man.

As for Lee, he felt that at any moment perhaps a messenger would appear shouting the order for a halt to the proceedings; that a reprieve had been granted – but no messenger appeared. What he believed to be a newly acquired "faith", through the visions he had just had, in the hope of a Divine rescue was rapidly slipping away, and so was any so-called inner peace.

Berry had taken centre stage now and was in command of the next part of the proceedings. He neatly placed the white sack over Lee's head finally eliminating any last glimmer of Earth's daylight, whilst an assistant pinioned his ankles. Lee trembled as Berry secured the sack into position around his neck with the rope – snugging the fatal "knot" somewhere below his right ear, then dashing for the large iron lever awaited the efficiently timed "amen" from the priest and corresponding nod from the prison governor.

Swinging on the large iron lever the expected sound of drawn bolts, the bursting yield of trapdoor and the shudder of the full weight of a man's body jolting to a sudden sickening stop should have brought everything to a close … but … Nothing!

If it were possible for silence to be deafening then this was one of those unique occasions. But it was not to last. Without further delay and almost as expected, Berry frantically attempted two more pulls on the large iron lever sending a mechanical shudder under the wooden planks which mysteriously only seemed to travel no further than the final linkages connecting the trap.

"Wha'… the … what's … what you doin' Berry … what's the hold up?" spluttered out the startled governor.

"How the hell do I know! Thiz summat wrong wi your damn contraption!" retorted Berry, frantically glaring and stomping around the platform hoping to find some obvious impediment which may have fouled the mechanism.

"Oh God! – look – quick somebody!" shouted the governor.

Seeing the condemned man beginning to waver like a reed in the wind Berry, plus two hefty officers, rushed to catch him before he fell in a heap on the trap half strangling himself in the process in an entangled rope.

"Get out the way you fat hulk," was about the best of politeness Berry could muster in the heat of the moment as he barged past the bewildered, babbling priest, towards the fainting man.

The whole hanging party was now in a state of disarray. The governor, sensing the need to exert his full-voice of authority, eventually brought the pandemonium to a sobering halt:

"Stop! Get him off … get him off! … And get Raife. Dammit! Where is that man, I want him here now … immediately!"

Quickly the two officers followed by the prison surgeon escorted Lee to a suitable space in a storage shed away from the scaffold whilst deciding what to do next.

A couple of hand-picked reporters had been permitted to observe the proceedings and they were frantically scribbling away at their notebooks whilst outside the prison gates small pockets of crowds stood nearby awaiting the confirmation that the execution had been administered.

Raife had by now been found and was being rushed across the prison yard looking somewhat disgruntled having been disturbed from his usual morning beverages.

"Get up here man – up here!" bawled the governor.

"… I thought you said this contraption of yours was in working order?"

"Ww … ot … what?" replied Raife in a now somewhat subdued and bewildered tone.

"Arr – arr 'twas workin' alroit yest'day sir," Raife replied as he nimbly scurried up onto the platform, wide eyed, looking closely at the trap.

"Olrioit sir … Mr Berry can you give her another try if ye would sir."

Without hesitation Berry had no sooner half swung on the iron lever when the trap burst open with swift ease.

"Damn it!" scethed Berry.

"What's this? Go on try ur again." Raife continued.

Swiftly, Berry repeated the action he'd tried only a few seconds earlier only to get the exact same results.

"Hmm …" shrugged Raife turning to an equally amazed set of onlookers.

"Donna think yer got any problems thure sirs … she seems a workin arlroit now yr know."

"Aye so it seems." chimed in Berry.

"… but summat wer foulin' t' trap … bet it wo that theer priest … bet 'e wo standin' on a loose boord or summat. Check it Raife, get thi sen down theer an' 'ave a look underneath, see if tha can find owt loose an all –"

"Err … I think we ought to resume as fast as we can Mr Berry," interrupted the Prison Governor fumbling his pocket timepiece.

"…We've wasted enough time on this. It's obvious that everything's working correctly now – I think we can all agree now can't we?" He gave reassuring glances to the two reporters whilst hoping to draw some nod of agreement from anyone else.

"… Good, that's it then," he continued, obviously assuming everyone else was in agreement.

"Let's have him back!"

Meanwhile Lee was being counselled by the priest and prison surgeon. Obviously dazed by the past experience Lee was not in any fit state to take in any lame excuses the two "counsellors" had to offer for the botched attempt made only a few minutes ago. But a decision had now been made to carry out a second attempt and the loud command from the prison governor to "have him back" had reached their ears and they'd got Lee standing to his feet in readiness.

What a pathetic pitiful sight it must have been to the two officers seeing Lee standing between them bent over and shaking like a frightened animal awaiting slaughter. Of course the white sack had been removed immediately after the first fiasco allowing Lee to breathe and even speak if he so wished, but of course he was so dazed by the event he could hardly splutter a word.

But then, out of the blue, he raised his previously bowed head and assumed an almost dignified stance; a strange unnatural poise almost resembling a new confidence seemed to take over him.

The two guards looked sceptically at each other; half relieved that the next part of their job would be without fierce resistance but also temporarily shocked by the unusual change. It seemed that Lee had gained some unexplained confidence and began to mutter those words he'd heard during one of those times spent with the plumber.

"Believe … J'John Babbacome Lee … believe … John Babbacome Lee … only believe … h-only believe"

At first his mutterings were hardly audible and muffled to the guards who weren't taking much notice, but John had become much calmer now and able to face his ordeal with an uncanny demeanour.

CHAPTER 5

JUSTICE – DELAYED OR DENIED ?

If chaos had erupted inside the prison walls it wasn't much better outside. Tension was running high now amongst the crowd of vengeance seekers and spectators who eagerly awaited the raising of the ominous black flag above the prison parapet indicating that justice had been satisfied. Crowd tension wasn't improved much either by the unusual buzz created by wide eyed journalists, frantically to-ing and fro-ing with their little note books and verbal innuendos to one another concerning the mysterious happenings within.

Of course the foundation of superstitious humbug had already been laid amongst the locals about Lee's calm demeanour in court; boldly claiming his innocence and that God would not let him hang. This only added to the atmosphere sending shudders of fear amongst the gullible; made worse when an isolated voice echoed the latest gleanings from the newspaper hounds.

"She's failed. The damn gallows has failed to work!" bawled a rather portly and obviously respected pillar of the community.

"They've had a couple of goes at hanging him now an' it's just not happened."

"What thi dooin then?" shreiked a voice from the crowd in response.

"Get to know! – get to know! – we demand to be informed. Surely they can't keep hangin' a bloke 'til thi pull his damn neck out!" shouted another.

A chilling wave of insecurity swept through the crowd leaving anything from murmurings of guilt to hushed nodding heads in confirmation of the plottings of witchcraft.

"Aye, told yer so," began the babblings amongst a small group of women.

"That there sister of 'is yer know was a bit of a dark 'un. Said she'd fix it olright fer 'im … reckon she's serves the other bloke yr know."

"What! Who? D' yer mean Ol' Nick?" piped up a young lass barely in her twenties.

"Aye ye got a lot t' learn about the ways o' folks round 'ere y' know lassy. I tell ye thrs not much gets past me an all wi'out me knowin'."

"Excuse me butting in," chimed up a rather cultured gentleman wearing a top hat, hardly giving an excuse for overhearing their conversation.

."But some of what you spoke of may have a grain of truth in it. As for the rest … well I'm not from these parts and so know little of your ways as you so put it.

However what I was about to comment on is this business of … err … well, let's see, what can we call it? let's say I believe this may have been caused by some other hand of fate as it were."

"Ooo aye … 'and of fate ye say? Goo on surr, what 'and of fate do ye mean an' all thaat?"

A few others had cottoned on to the conversation by now and a small group had stolen away from the main forum discussing the prison catastrophe.

"Well I wouldn't go as far as to reduce it to fate, but perhaps shall we say … Divine Providence."

"Ooo yr giving me the eebi-jeebiz now surr , but go on!"

"Well I don't know if you've come across what might be little more than a spot of sensationalism, but recently one of our nearby villages had one of those new revival type church meetings. Now don't quote me on this but apparently the man preaching was some Yorkshire chap who did a few miracles, or at least the Man upstairs did as he claimed."

A bland silent expression hung on some of the faces with sceptically matching glances.

"Err yes?" commented a voice. And what's this got to do with Lee right now today?"

The gentleman pondered a while in order to give himself a chance to select the right words in response.

"Well, as I say some Yorkshire chap, one of those evangelist types you know – gives a hearty sermon apparently, plus prayers for the sick which … err … seem to get results."

Rubbing the back of his head, as if to partly distract himself from any look of embarrassment, the stranger went on:

"In fact I'd heard about him and being in the area for a few days I thought I'd nip in one evening, just out of curiosity mind, to one of his meetings. I must say,

I was told something from one of the folk there which really shook me –"

The stranger was just about to make an important point when suddenly he was sharply interrupted by an angry chilling wail from a plump, very rude and vocal, yet well-dressed woman wearing a blue tightly fitting undersized bonnet causing her furiously pink cheeks to bulge abnormally, squeezing her dark eyes into a combined piercing glare.

"Poppycock! Poppycock young man! I've seen charlatans like him before – think they can heal folks by the touch of the hand an' all – read too much Bible I think. Hypocrites! Think they're Jesus or someone. As far as I 'm concerned they're all rogues!"

Had it not been for the larger part of the crowd one would have anticipated a silent pause at that very moment and a fertile vacuum for questions and comments. But too much was going on, and more and more attention was being given to other more relevant opinions about the hold up in the administration of justice.

Not only that but heated differences were rising to almost flash point amongst some of the disembarked fishermen who had decided to sample the local alms-house produce whilst making the whole event a day out for the lads. An enforcement of "Peelers" had been drafted to help quell the pending riot. It was as if the whole structure of civil order had momentarily failed; what had seemingly defied the Law on the inside of the prison gates was rapidly percolating through to the outer community.

Back inside the situation was no better, in fact it was worse. Poor John Lee had been placed in a side room whilst more inspection of the contraption took place. Berry was completely beside himself by now. Nobody had ever witnessed him in a state like this before – ever. Like a man possessed he began foaming at the mouth and ranting in what was a mixture of Yorkshire curses and expletives plus slurred gibberish which was utterly incomprehensible. As a hefty man Berry was almost unstoppable when he got into one of his psychotic rages and woe betide anyone who tried to physically restrain him. Some had often heard about his explosive seizures but had put it down to just another temper burst common to most. But this was different. Totally beside himself Berry had flung himself onto the rope and bounced his hefty force onto the trap causing it to spring and judder in response. Would it have opened? Who knows? Berry didn't care; he was going to burst the damn thing open to kill or cure, whether he went into the hole himself or not.

Meanwhile the onlookers stood back in fear of what this man might do next.

Taking advantage of a moment of exhaustion in Berry's outburst the governor spoke in a somewhat reconciling tone:

"Right, quietly gather yourselves folks, resume your positions, we are to try a third and final time."

Eventually Lee was brought back in and an eerie calm settled the storm's eye on the scaffold ensemble. It was almost as if a switch had been turned; Berry was back to his calm almost "reverend" self as if he'd been unaware of the scene he'd just created.

CHAPTER 6

THRICE SHE TRY AND THRICE SHE FAIL!

Right this is it! Berry hissed to himself, clenching his teeth in a contorted grimace. *I'm gonna hang that slippery little toe-rag now if it kills me! I've never failed before, and I'll not fail today so help me ... God!*

Quite often Berry would resort to some twisted version of scripture to bolster his hypocritical piety whenever humiliated, and this occasion was no exception – far worse, belligerent outburst well packaged within a flustered Yorkshire dialect sometimes became so incomprehensible that his foul language almost became more entertaining than offensive. So articulate when swearing; if you could call it articulate, Berry could wittily cram so many obscene expletives into one sentence that by the time he'd reached his "full-stop" the sentence had virtually lost its meaning. He could also split words up, slipping in yet more "adjectives" to give his expression even more colour – a skill that only a northerner, schooled in the art of coal mining parlance could engineer.

Berry had momentarily calmed himself down somewhat since his previous rant of "fuffing and puffing" and was now ready, needless to say, determined to finish the job.

A rude silence gripped the whole pantomime with an atmospheric tension more akin to a standoff at a gunfight than what should have been the serious composure of the administration of justice. The troupe had swiftly located position yet again ready to get it over and done with, nervously eyeballing each other in anticipation of the next move. The expression in their rapidly oscillating eyes said it all: flickering first on Lee, Berry, the governor, then Berry again, his fingers eagerly tickling the large iron trigger. The fat priest was no exception; twitching and hovering in his white cassock from one toe to the next he rather resembled a large balloon dressed in a parachute, creating a buoyant oversize, much to the irritation of the two guards who were reluctantly cajoling the condemned man. In reality no one really wanted this; neither did they want to prolong it.

There was blame to be placed somewhere – but where and on whom to pin it? This should not have happened; something or rather someone was at fault for such a failure to have taken place, and everyone was under suspicion. Raife, the mechanic, might have been an obvious choice but vowed and declared that all was working perfectly as was demonstrated both before the "execution" and again after the two botched attempts. And now responsibly placed beneath the scaffold platform in order to immediately deal with any mechanical failure it could hardly make him a suspect. Yet the failure was mechanical, that was obvious. Could the prison guards have hindered proceedings somehow? And what about the priest whose sheer weight on the platform plus his excited jiggling about, might have caused one of the floor planks to momentarily shift and jam the trap? Could it have been part of a plot to save Lee; a conspired plan? Could even friends of that shifty lawyer friend of Miss Keyes have had a lucrative influence somewhere within the higher echelons of the prison governing body?

One thing seems pretty sure, Berry seemed the least suspect; to him a hanging was worth £10 plus expenses – failure was not an option. Or was some unforeseen hand at work over which man had no control? They were soon to find out.

Suddenly the flashing exchange of glances ended in combined focus with a throat- clearing sound from the governor – the signal to prepare.

The priest momentarily stopped hovering in order to give aim to the last line of the prayer of committal from which his AMEN would signal the two supporting guards to quickly stand aside, and signal the governor to give the final nod to Berry.

And so it came; swinging mightily on the iron lever Berry heartily responded to the governor's nod. As the shackles, rods and linkages tensioned in obedience to the lever's squeaky thrust, the heavy draw-bolts yielded their support from the deadly oak trap door with a positive "clunk".

And ... it was over ... it was ... was ... it was stuck! *"What!?"* About two inches of movement and that was it!

Ghastly encircled wide eyes seeking an answer and speechless expressions captured a picture of utter and total disbelief – she'd failed!

Yet again the cursed trap had refused to open. A silence sat hanging for an eternity holding the assembled temporarily frozen to the spot; all save the poor wretch quivering with knees slowly buckling under his slumping upper weight, eventually having to be re-propped by the nearest guard.

Suddenly the thickening silence was rudely shattered by a guttural wail from the governor's voice.

"What the hell is happening down there?... Damn you Raife! ... What th'... force it man ... force the damn thing! … Ah ... gain ... Berry... again - again ... give it another swing."

Berry frantically burst into action with gusto in response, arms and legs powerfully poised, the hangman swung the iron lever to and fro like a clumsy pendulum; *eek- ha- eek-ha- eek-ah-eek,* back and forth squeaked the crude iron trigger ending its momentum with a foul outburst from the executioner.

The pace now quickened; spiralling into organised chaos the shambolic set jumped and stomped around on what might be offending floor boards giving the whole shebang more resemblance to an Indian war dance than an execution. Berry was ranting on the lever. The two guards who initially had to step back were half on and half off the trap door trying to prop the poor sap from keeling over through fainting whilst at the same time running great risk of falling through the hole themselves– all three together – when and if the trap should perform. The prison surgeon had his head in his hands, whilst the fat priest had impulsively stepped back in fear of some divine retribution only to give himself a backward flip over the scaffold steps ending like an inverted turtle into the yard's open water tank – face reddened with repentant embarrassment.

"God help us!" cried the governor.

"Stop! Stop! For God's sake stop! Enough, this is enough – final!

Thrice she try and thrice she fail. Get him off ... get him off ... take him down immediately ... today's event is over", continued the governor, his voice fading in submissive relief.

The governor was aware of the need to step in fast amidst what was turning into a fiasco. He was all too aware of Berry's antics during the last episode and feared what he might do if he were to suddenly snap into one of his gymnastic style lunges at the trap hoping to win the day. But the governor had little to fear as by now Berry had exhausted himself into a gentle slithering down the wooden well -greased lever mount, until he sat almost contemplative, half cross legged on the scaffold deck; he had failed – he had given up, and now sat dazed in a melancholy stupor hardly muttering a word.

Then, as if things couldn't get any worse fate herself mocked a curt gesture – the trap-door flung wide open affirming a distinct "clomp" as it smacked firm against the wooden stopper. But Lee had gone; in seconds after stepping away between two guards the infernal contraption worked as if there was nothing wrong at all.

With jaw dropped in shock and mouth already wide open the governor expelled his charged lungs with such a vehement gust that all the day's frustration was released into one throat wrenching word:

"Raaaa ... aiff !!"... and it came right from his toenails.

"Where the hell are you? c'm'ere ... now!"

If the governor was expecting to see Raife's greasy cap pop up through the trap hole any second then he was about to be disappointed; Raife had vanished – gone!

"Excuse me sir," politely interrupting a softening voice from the under-sheriff standing at some distance in the prison yard.

"But it appears that Mr ... err ... Raife as you call him, had to abandon his post in rather a hurry."

"What?" retorted the Governor.

"The privy sir ... the lavatory, apparently he became somewhat indisposed rather quickly."

"Indisposed, what do you mean?"

"I don't know sir, but he did seem quite desperate as he shot past me sir."

"Desperate! ... desperate! ... I'll give him desperate ... find him somebody... find him."

A few minutes passed before one of the officials hailed across the yard:

"Here sir... found him, but I think he'll need a doctor ... he looks pretty grim."

"Go an' have a look doc," said the governor nonchalantly flipping his hand towards the prison surgeon in response. There were far more important things than Raife to worry about now.

The charade was coming to an end. John Babbacome Lee would not hang today – or at any other time. Lee now sat in his cell, awaiting a decision about his fate – a reprieve? One could hope. Penal servitude was a more likely outcome but all this would need a decision from the Home Office; a process that would not happen in five minutes. When the surgeon examined the prisoner he was shocked to find the ordeal had uncannily taken its toll. Sitting hunched on the cell floor, hugging his knees in a slow rocking back and forth motion, Lee had more resemblance to a man twice his age than the cocky youth of only a few weeks ago.

Meanwhile the governor had become acutely aware of another problem which needed immediate and skilful address. There was a growing mob gathering outside the prison gates eager to know whether or not justice had been satisfied; the absence of the black flag meant something had not gone entirely to plan – they were demanding an explanation. Because it was late in the morning and noon was fast approaching, it meant that any local newspaper reporters might just be able to meet the deadline for the evening news – the pressure was on.

Without further delay, realising the need for a brief but satisfactory response, the Governor and Under-Sheriff made haste toward the main building hoping to cobble together a written statement with which the Under-Sheriff could use to address the crowd. Finally the reluctant duo braced themselves; making their way towards the main prison gate.

CHAPTER 7

BERRY GOES HOME

Depression had often found its home in the demoralised Berry, and right now it had cloaked him heavily. With eager passion to get out of Exeter as soon as possible; heaving himself forward through the busy streets of the town he rushed towards the train station which would swiftly race him out of sight and mind back to his home roots in Bradford.

Rounding a street corner on which stood a well fronted chapel, his concentration was suddenly disturbed by what he could only describe as a holy rumpus from within. Hearty shouts and euphoric bursts of: "Hallelujah! Praise the Lord!" from what was an obviously well charged atmosphere brought Berry up sharp as curiosity got the better of him. Peering through curtained entrance on the inner doorway, Berry had mysteriously found himself in the vestibule. Much to his surprise he was met by sights of people with arms high in the air, singing praying heartily with angelic eloquence, some lying prostrate on the floor, whilst an all too familiar preacher was booming forth in good old fashioned hell fire style. Berry felt fixed to the spot. Had he wanted to move he couldn't have. His immediate recognition of the preacher inwardly gave him urge to make a swift retreat but his legs failed to respond. Berry knew only too well that the man holding forth was the famous Smith Wigglesworth from Bradford – the same city as the infamous hangman, James Berry. By strange coincidence both men of notoriety lived in the same city and little more than half a mile apart. Both were about the same age; both Yorkshire men, yet totally opposite, especially in profession.

Smith Wigglesworth was an outstanding preacher, to say the least. A humble plumber from Bradford who couldn't read or write until he was twenty seven was totally sold out to the Gospel, and was a man of profound faith. One couldn't help being influenced by this man's presence. Powerfully charismatic pioneer of the new Pentecostal movement, signs and wonders followed this man wherever he went. A man with a mission, Wigglesworth had no time for small-talk and niceties. Sometimes he could be brash, even rude according to some, but his results were indeed astonishing. When one witnessed Wigglesworth in action it was like being swept back into a scene from the New Testament age of the Apostles. He had faith to move mountains and a compassion that would take him to the ends of the earth if it meant he could rescue the vilest of sinners from eternal damnation – such was this man's zeal.

Suddenly the humble plumber swung into action. It was almost as if he knew Berry was gingerly peering through the doorway curtain.

"No matter how much good you think you've done in your life. No matter how many religious acts you've performed, if you don't know the Lord Jesus Christ as your personal Saviour you're lost – you're bound!"

He laid such emphasis on the word "bound," it was a miracle in itself that half the congregation didn't get blown out of their seats by his sheer vocal gust.

He went on to say how trying to keeping the letter of the law is nothing more than "religious clap trap" to God and what He really requires is a pure and contrite heart.

Berry had now backed himself into a gap between the door frame and a rather hefty set of drawers, wedging himself into yet further immobility. The preacher had touched on a spot which caused something to stir within him.

"Law! … law," Berry murmured to himself. What does he know about law? I know more about that than him. Don't I carry out its justice; doing God's work, isn't that my ministry?"

Berry was beginning to react. He knew only too well that his legalistic worldview was being challenged, and right to the core.

"The Bible tells us that we have all fallen short of the glory of God, none of us deserve 'eaven. Jesus was the expressed image of the Father and what the law couldn't do Jesus did – fulfilment of the law ... a new law ... a scandal of grace! He took your punishment; my punishment on that cross so all we have to do is accept it … it's a gift … All we 'ave to do is come to Jesus with a repentant 'eart and accept it … be set free now from the curse of sin and death – because whoever the Son sets free is free indeed … It's a gift! Grace! … Grace! … Grace! … Jesus was the epitome of grace!"

The preacher boomed on.

At this point Berry almost burst. Wigglesworth was now looking straight at him as if his eyes had landed a direct hit through the gap in the curtain, despite Berry's temporary hideout squeezed next to the chest of drawers.

"Grace! What?" muttered Berry to himself.

"I've no time for any soppy get out. Wrongdoers deserve punishment and that's it. That's where we differ Wiggy, I'm not having a plumber telling me about justice! *Eye for an eye, tooth for tooth, life for life* – isn't that what it says in that book of yours? Sinners are responsible for their own sins – get what they deserve – eh!"

"Honly believe! … Honeley believe! ... All things are possible, honly believe!"

The preacher boomed again.

"Listen at him."

The inner struggle became even fiercer now; his whole fabric was welling up into vehement hatred towards the preacher.

"Can't even speak right … honly believe, honly believe, 'oley 'oley 'oley Lord God Almighty! Somebody tell him where the H's go in a sentence! What school did he go to, if any?"

Berry was really being challenged now. Still raw from his failure to administer what he called God's justice, any idea of a wrongdoer being set free wound him up intensely, and it certainly couldn't have come at a worse time to hear a preacher barking on about grace! In Berry's experience as a lawman there was no grace, the nearest might be mercy which a judge and court alone could administer on delivery of sentence, after that justice must be satisfied and that was it. John Lee had been found guilty and should have paid the penalty, but somehow had slipped the noose. Inwardly this bothered Berry and only added to his inner turmoil and what would later turn out to have a direct consequence on his mental state.

"Get out Berry! Get out!"

Suddenly a sharp inner voice crackled in his head. Berry spun round expecting to find someone standing behind him or to one side – but no one was there.

Best get out now eh whilst you've chance, the voice went on.

Perhaps he was talking to himself, either way it seemed like a good idea.

You'll miss your train, again with subtle whisper.

Nicely coinciding with a pause in the proceedings during which time a young lady with a large hat had positioned herself on the platform ready to sing, Berry saw his chance to escape. The subtlety of the idea of "missing the train" also shocked him enough to break free from his "frozen" spot in the corner and make his exit. Just as he had gained release from his anchorage and turning to the door, the lady heartily struck up with the opening line of that famous hymn *Amazing Grace*. That was just about the last straw! Wide eyed and back stiffly arched with both arms flapping uncontrollably, it was if the startled Berry had given himself a large boot up the backside as he swiftly jettisoned himself like a rocket through the chapel door way. Half skidding down the slippery stone steps he landed in a heap on the wet pavement outside with his legs flailing in the air like a windmill, giving mild entertainment to a hand full of passers-by and feeling just about as stupid as one could get. But he was out, and that was all that mattered.

"Best head for the station, quick!" he gasped to himself.

Picking himself up and trying to dust off as much embarrassment as he could from himself he made haste for the station.

"Ooh damn! That hurt!"

Nursing what was becoming an increasing awareness of injury his feeling of stupidity was rapidly giving way to a rather bruised and wet backside.

"Oooh, best get a move on before any of those Bible thumpers swoop on an easy target and try some laying on of hands healing stuff or get me saved or something."

Berry hobbled on, picking up pace as the pain wore off.

Berry's arrival at the station found him somewhat flustered. He was late. His train to Bristol was already waiting, hissing on the opposite platform. He was on the wrong side.

Damn! he thought. *I'll never make it, I'll have to go over the footbridge to get to the other side o' t' flamin' rail track!*

The pressure was on. With new desperation he pressed on by the ticket office window hastily wheezing, puffing and heart pounding, his boots clumsily clanged their way along the iron stairway of the railway bridge, finally to deliver a panic stricken red faced Berry on the platform at the other side.

Quick now, just through the porters gate and I'll be there, he thought to himself.

But contrary to his hopes it wasn't going to be quite as smooth as he thought. Just has he rounded the passageway next to the porter's office he was confronted by a large baggage trolley manned by two burly porters blocking the way. This wouldn't normally have been a major obstacle; usually one could find a means of squeezing past one way or another – especially in a hurry, but the realisation of something far worse suddenly hit him like a thunderbolt! On seeing the pile of baggage Berry winced to an abrupt halt. Body stiffening with shock he realised he had left his important leather bag in the chapel vestibule as a result of his swift exit.

"Ahgh! No!"

Clenched fists in the air, and the guttural sounds from this large man gave the porters such a fright that one of them tripped backwards over a mail sack, landing himself between the trolley and the wall creating a further blockage in the passageway and eliminating any hope of Berry climbing through.

"No!" he went on.

The other porter looked on in amazement.

"Are you alright sir?" he asked.

Berry suddenly calmed himself so as to reduce any further embarrassment and attention from people on the platform.

"Sorry… sorry, only I've just realised I've come without my damn bag!"

"Oh dear" the porter replied. "Well perhaps if you leave some forwarding details we can help retrieve it for you sir."

"Err, y' yes that'll be – "

Berry was just about to take the porter up on his idea when he was interrupted by the guard blowing his whistle for the train to pull out of the station. Realising that his hopes of getting out of Exeter to safe haven up North were about to vanish very quickly, a decision was imperative. To turn round and go back to the chapel was impossible now if he was going to catch this train. The next one might be the following day or even later – *too much of a risk* he thought to himself, in any case being swamped by a load of hyped evangelicals whilst trying to explain himself was unthinkable.

Reading Berry's dilemma, the startled porter had by now recovered from his position between the trolley and the wall and was able to provide Berry with enough gap to squeeze through and bolt for the train. With his Mackintosh cape flying in the air behind him like the wings of a bat, Berry chased the moving locomotive and just in the nick of time to grab a brass carriage door handle – any door – give it a quick twist open and in!

Berry settled himself down to the comfort of a plush compartment seat as the train pulled out of the station. However, in the chaos, Berry had wrongly placed himself in 1st class, but he didn't care, if he had to move he would; until then was happy to just stay put. He was quite alone which gave him just the privacy he needed to gather his thoughts, rest his tired body, and reflect on the past forty eight hours.

CHAPTER 8

THE JOLLY JACK TAR

Meanwhile back in Exeter, Berry had indeed left behind quite a trail of excitement. The botched hanging had fuelled plentiful amounts of gossip and there was one pub in particular that was always a good place to get a good news update – *The Jolly Jack Tar*. The *"Jack"*, as the locals preferred to call it, was to say the least a bit of a dive. To call it an alms house was an insult to pubs in general. Smoke filled saloons and sawdust floors; spittoons and loud cackling hags, with clay pipes, having had their day in the "profession" could be seen happily apprenticing young fillies in the lucrative art of "room service" for many a salty sea-dog seeking the solace of a fair maid after a long time at sea. Raucous sailors, copious flagons of scrumpy cider plus hearty sea shanties to an accompanying piano and fiddle player, created a unique camaraderie. The spirit of the place was certainly unique and despite the low-life of the place, one looked after one's mate. Nearly all had a sordid past of one sort or another which gave common bond to the house; but having said all that you didn't trust anyone completely. Things could turn without warning – Landlord and Lady always keeping an eye on any new faces who might cause trouble.

The *Jack* was convenient for sailors of all rank and breed although Navy officers usually gave the place a wide berth, either to turn a blind eye to unruly deck-hands or simply just to find somewhere more select. They usually came up on the river Exe's tidal flood which gave them about twelve hours or so to enjoy the town of Exeter until the tidal cycle reappeared its same height again, and then turning on an ebb flow would nicely take them back down stream to the port.

It was on this occasion that they had previously arrived during the morning tide and were able to join in the hysterics of the crowd outside the prison. Having later been dispersed by the "Peelers" before any real trouble started to brew, the seamen had drifted into town for the forenoon's last tipple - a bite to eat to soak up the ale, ready for a good evening session at the *Jack,* to where they would eventually gravitate around sunset. And so they arrived.

On hearing their approaching racket outside in the street as they neared the door, the landlord began cautiously clearing any loose glasses and bottles from the bar. He also gave a warning nod to a few of his trusted mates, including the established pianist who was well used to the technique of switching the tune or tempo appropriately, creating any positive change of mood which might defuse a hostile atmosphere. But then the patrons were well used to all this and quite often seadogs and landlubbers alike would eventually unite in their common interest of swilling down large quantities of ale, cider or porter as their tastes and customs required – jigging along to a crude, noisy musical background.

And so the place had its own methods of dealing with scoundrels, and the landlord was usually able to keep the lid on things before anything got out of hand. He realised that too much reliance on the Law might damage "trade" as the *Jack* had become a steady "silk-road" for the odd movement of contraband from time to time. The police were quite happy to keep a tolerant relationship more or less on the basis: "don't bother us and we'll not bother you", until of course someone really pushed it, and then enforced customs officers would come down on hard-line smugglers like a ton of bricks.

Suddenly a rather well-oiled swarthy member of the gathering took a swiping lunge at what appeared to be an ale-soaked crumpled newspaper on one of the wooden tables in front of him. At first, the sudden swift movement took the immediately surrounding fraternity by surprise, causing some to step back sharply thinking a live fist might be about to engage. But what he'd seen, in spite of his drunken state, was about to change the whole atmosphere of the pub. Clumsily unfolding the front page as he wobbled on his feet he attempted to blubber out a semi-coherent string of words which sounded more like a flushing toilet than a verbal sentence.

"Eee—h joost look a' tha' will ye", he slurred.

Barely able to understand what he was trying to say, his companions were now focussing on the headlines of the "Exeter Evening News".

"BABBACOMBE MAN CHEATS GALLOWS" There it was; a published report of the day's event.

"Aye we know all about thaat dunna we, we were all outside the prison gates this morn … worn't we?" chuckled one of the hags puffing on her clay pipe.

"That's right ... three times they tried an' all … Didn't work though," noddingly agreed one of the group.

"That maybe, but they reckon his hair turned white in minutes ye know… reckon he looks twice his age now."

"Arr … like an old man," said another.

"Hey look ye here … says he's awaitin' a decision from the 'ome office … what to do with 'im … reckon they'll give 'im another hangin' again Spike?" said one of the more sober members peering over the wobbling drunk's shoulder.

"Let's 'ave a look," replied Spike rudely snatching the newspaper from the drunk's hands.

"Hmm … according to this it looks as if he might get a life sentence … hmm … can't hang a man more than three times ... 'tis the Law ye know – ."

"Ah but what's that say?" interrupted a scurvy looking sea –dog pushing his mattered beard between Spike's face and the paper.

"He could get akk … akseted, it says … What's that?… Axed … that's it ... does that mean they gonna chop 'is 'ead off ?"

"No you fool," replied Spike, sharply recoiling from the foul plume of the man's breath.

"The word's acquitted! It means they could let him off … you brainless duffer!"

By now a fair gathering was beginning to give attention to the news of the day as they stood or sat around the tables near the crackling log fire away from the winter's draughts.

"What I would like to know is what actually happened ... what caused it to fail, because to me it looks like sabotage?" piped up a tall stranger leaning on the fire mantle, puffing a pipe.

"Maybe that half-sister and her dodgy lawyer friend had something to do with it ... I reckon they rigged the gallows," said Spike.

"Ahhh! More like witchcraft," chimed in one of the hags eager to have her say.

"Shut up you ignorant peasant," came a curt remark from one of the group.

"Aye, clear off! An' take yer broomstick with ye ... hee he!" added Spike.

A chorus of tittering chuckles echoed around the small gathering in response.

"Excuse me 'scuse me," interrupted the landlady as she bustled her way through the cluster of bodies, carrying a substantially large pie.

"Need to put me supper near the fire for a while ... gotta keep things warm ye know on a night like this."

"Aye oo arr," came a murmuring tone in agreement.

"Keep yer eye on it will ye? And mind that mangy dog of yours will ye Rip ... don't want that mut near my cookin'."

By now the group had re-shuffled themselves after making way for the landlady. The stranger had placed himself in a prominent position half sitting and leaning on one of the stone flags by the large fireplace, nursing a tankard of ale close to his chest, and seemed eager to add comment.

"Well you might laugh and ridicule some of those things but I reckon there could be a bit of truth in what the old woman just said."

A silent pause hung for a few moments leaving bewildered expressions on faces. And then one by one they began to laugh mockingly thinking it was a joke.

"No, no, no I'm serious ... let me explain."

Suddenly the mocking sniggers died down as they began to give attention to the stranger's assertive tone, wondering what he was going to say next. Taking a last sup from his ale tankard he continued:

"Well it's like this you see. I was also up there amongst the crowd outside the prison, when I happened to hear a rather well educated gentleman, wearing a top hat, say something about a preacher in the area. Unfortunately he got interrupted by a rather rude woman in a silly bonnet. But anyway I managed to catch up with him later and he was able to tell me a bit more. Apparently the preacher was a Yorkshire-man called Smith or something – not quite sure but it doesn't matter – but he could really draw a crowd.

Some folk, they reckon, had experienced miraculous healings which had astounded even the physicians. Some say … dare I say it ... he'd even raised the dead! The point being is, that they reckon he'd had a bit to do with Miss Keyes and even prophesied to that young scoundrel Lee, who worked for her, that he *only had to believe and he would be saved.* Now saved from what I'm not sure, but it does make you think doesn't it? Especially when the scoundrel stood up in court and said, *God will not let me hang*?"

By now the stranger had the full attention of just about the whole pub, except that is for old Rip who was more interested in the landlady's pie than the story. Rip was an old soldier whose hard life had taught him to survive. He usually kept body and soul together doing a spot of fishing, poaching and general wheeling and dealing as chance smiled on him – a cunning plan was beginning to hatch.

Suddenly the pensive atmosphere was shattered.

"Damn you Punch! Get out of here!" Without warning Rip swung his boot at the Jack Russell, flicking Punch's chubby little backside so high in the air that the rest of the poor dog spun head over heels in windmill fashion skittling a pile of bottles on a far window seat.

"I'm sorry Ma but I'm afraid me dog's pissed on yer pie," said Rip sheepishly looking towards the landlady.

It wasn't the first time crafty old Rip had played this trick in other pubs further afield, and both dog and master were well used to the routine, as was evident by what seemed almost like a cocky smirk on Punch's face as he perched quite unperturbed on the window seat, looking back at his master as if it was all in a day's work. Rip had seized the moment. Whilst the rest were so engrossed in the stranger's story he'd sneakily tipped some of his ale onto the piecrust in order to give the desired effect.

"Don't worry Ma I think I can save most of it. The bad bit I'll chuck in the river on me way out," he continued, skilfully taking a knife and cutting a nice portion – scooping it into his readily opened, large ditty bag.

Quickly handing the remaining pie to the angry looking landlady he made haste towards the door before she'd chance to explode.

The sudden disturbance brought an abrupt end to the evening's topic; the seamen were starting to disperse in order to catch the ebb tide, the Publicans were about to call time, and Punch and his master were looking forward to a home-cooked supper.

CHAPTER 9

THE VISITOR

S everal months had now passed since the Exeter foul-up and slowly Berry was beginning to recover from the shattering events, and trying to get back to his usual routine.

The Berry household was about the same as any other family in Bradford, complete with all the usual ups and downs that life brings along when raising children. During the early years James had held a professional position as a police constable but as the need to provide more and more for his family grew he found himself pursuing various business ventures, including working on a patent in his attic workshop in the hope of its becoming a viable sideline. Of course dreams like that take time, but in the meantime I suppose it was nice to have a viable hobby.

It was during one of his leaner times whilst working as a shoe salesman that he came across the advert for a job as executioner – something which he had never really contemplated. However, he had become friendly with the famous William Marwood, and as a genuine "student" had been privileged to assist Mr Marwood in the administration of his art on the odd occasion. Being thus "apprenticed", James Berry had seized the opportunity for a career move and with it a better income. Of course breadwinner was one thing – executioner was another.

The Berry's had already moved from one address at Bilton Place due to the neighbours taking a dislike to living next to a man whose job was "killing people for a living" and were now at Cliffe Road; no longer tenant but owner. His new career plus a little "fame" for having an unusual job opened up many a lecture engagement, sometimes albeit with "magic lantern" slides for a professional touch, yielding that little extra on the side for his pocket. In an uncanny way as time went on he had also managed to earn some respect (as well as a spot of that extra cash) as a professional who in reality was only carrying out a constitutional legal punishment which was representative of the democratic wishes of all concerned. After all he was only the last link in the long chain of legal administrational duty; voted in place by Parliament for public security, and whether people liked it or not, the burden of taking a life rested on everyone – it was just that Berry had the rotten job of carrying it out.

Did Berry like his job? Well in short – no! In fact sometimes he positively hated it. Occasionally when about to set off for a new appointment his wife would have to cajole him through the door against a tirade of reasons he could think up for why he ought not to go. One can imagine the mood swings this job of his could create. Being a hangman was fine for the money, but what usually kept him sane was the belief that he was carrying out the wishes of God and country; ridding the nation of ghastly vermin so people could all sleep safely in their beds, but at what a cost. If people only knew what it was like to take another human being's life in such a cold and calculated manner.

If life seemed good on the outside, on the inside it was not all it was cracked up to be, and often Mrs Berry, whom the whole family called Ma, would find herself "walking on egg-shells" whenever her husband walked through the door after a day "at work".

One day James came home after giving one of his evening lectures in one of the local pubs only to be met by an unusual atmosphere.

"Hello dearest ... had a good evening ... went well then?" said his wife, rather nervously smiling, making extra effort to welcome her husband.

"Aye, canna grumble" said James slowly squeezing off his boots half perched on a low wooden hearth stool.

"Well I've put the kids to bed an' got yer some supper in t' oven love – Hot Pot, y'r favourite. Now sit thi sen down now an' I'll serve it out."

She gently directing him towards the table with her hand on his shoulder.

"Makin' a bit of a fuss are'nt we lass ... summat up? Hey yer not expectin' again are yer?"

"Hee hee no no flower ... just in a good mood, really. I feel top of the world today ... had a visitor."

"Oo aye, anyone we know?" responded James, easing himself off the low stool in order to hang his coat on the door.

"Err … sit to the table hubby, let me get you some Hot-Pot and I'll tell you all about it," she replied leaving an intrigued look on her husband's face.

Sarah proceeded to carefully lift the stew-pot from the fireside cooking range onto a suitable place in the middle of the table. By now the savoury aroma had reached James's nose as he sat in relaxed expectation, peering towards his wife with a grateful smile. Gently ladling two handsome helpings of the steamy stew into James's bowl the exchange of glances said it all: Ma's' cooking wins their hearts every time.

Eagerly spooning down his favourite stew, James had almost forgotten about the visitor, but a momentary pause in the relish when asking his wife for a "spot more bread" gave him a short interval to re-cap on her previous comments.

"Go on then lass, tell us what's put t' wind in yer sails today pet, can't wait to know," he said munching on a freshly gravy dipped chunk of bread.

"Well," she gingerly began. "Can you remember telling me that you'd lost your bag when you'd been on that job in Exeter recently?"

"Umm aye," replied James still chomping the piece of bread.

"Well someone picked it up, and because you were wise enough to put your name and address in it, it found its way home."

James suddenly stopped eating, staring blankly towards the far end of the table.

"Are you alright dearest?" Sarah said, caressing the nape of her husband's neck.

He had almost gone into a daydream as his mind flashed back to the incident when he fell down the chapel steps, leaving his bag behind in his haste to get to Exeter train station.

"It's all right love," she continued. "There's no need to worry. Everything's there alright ... I mean, he was a lovely man who brought it, very kind ... in fact there was just something about him and what he said that really ... well ... set me aglow."

James Berry suddenly stopped eating – expressionless, now staring directly towards her. He wanted to know more but somehow feared who this strange visitor might be.

"G-, go on lass," he hesitantly responded fumbling for another chunk of bread.

"Well he'd been in Exeter himself," she began to explain. "And because he also lived in Bradford – I mean what a wonderful coincidence – he brought the bag back himself. Wasn't that kind of him?"

Berry just kept looking, giving a half nod towards his wife indicating that he wished her to tell more.

"And guess what. He says he doesn't live too far away from us; as a matter of fact I think he's the man who has something to do with that Gospel Mission on err ... what's it street – "

"Well who was he? What was the visitor's name?" he sharply interrupted.

"Name? Oh err… yes err ... a funny sort of name ... aye that's it …Wigglesworth, Mr Wigglesworth, that's it ... why do you think you know him?"

Now Berry had just made the mistake of slipping another piece of gravy soaked bread into his already wide-gaping mouth, and, on hearing the name "Wigglesworth", he gave a sharp intake of breath which caused a substantial crust to wedge itself into the back of his throat. Flapping and gurgling like a throttled duck; back arched and arms and legs splaying in desperation for air, the red faced choking man, was almost at tipping point over the back of the chair. In a flash his wife gave him such a whack between his shoulders that his projectile response not only sent the soggy crust hurtling across the room but brought Berry crashing forward, face down, towards the table. Naturally his arms and hands got there a split second first in order to save his face from splattering the bowl of stew, only to exacerbate the situation all the more. His thumb had caught the rim of the enamel dish sending it flipping through the air like a paddle wheel spraying a whirl of stew in the air and then landing upside down on the red tiled floor with a final metallic "clop!" Needless to say the stippling meat, potatoes, gravy and carrots, not to mention a few soggy bread crumbs made a nice, almost decorative pattern on the kitchen wall and ceiling.

"Lord above!" exclaimed his wife. "What in the world happened there? Are you alright love? Here let me get you a mug o' watter flower," she went on sympathetically rubbing the back of his neck.

The exhausted James took a sip of water slowly aiding his recovery and soothing his wrenched throat. Turning to his wife, reddened eyes still slightly bulging from the ordeal, he attempted to croak out a few words:

"Ah … ah … I don't want tha' man 'ere woman ... un'stand?"

Sarah looked bewildered. "Why dear, he's meant n' harm?"

He took another sip of water and by now his voice was regaining some normality.

"'Cos he's a fanatic, in fact they're all fanatics down there ... Bowland Street yer mean?" Sarah nodded.

"Aye, 'ave 'eard about it from folks who live near there ... reckon they jump about and dance a lot, cockin' their legs up in t' air and lookin' daft, then fall flat on t' floor reckoning its God's power or summat. Nah! Not for me that's not religion."

Berry shook his head in firm disapproval of what his wife might be getting drawn into.

"But James love, that's hearsay. They do an awful lot o' good down there and have helped a lot of needy folk get their lives back on t' rails, in fact I really wouldn't mind goin' and havin' a look myself outta curiosit – "

Suddenly Berry banged his fist on the table, abruptly stopping her in mid-sentence.

"Now listen here woman! We're brought up chapel, married in chapel an' that's it! It wor good enough for my parents an' it's good enough for thee lass. We're proper Christians in this house, none o' that fancy stuff 'ere ... so don't thee come with any of them daft ideas ... and that's final!"

Ma responded to her husband's command in quiet obedience and started to clear the table. A noticeable silence hung for a while giving each one space for calm and a chance for Ma to freshen the atmosphere with a change of subject.

"I'll just wipe some of this stew off the wall pet, before it crusts hard," she said in a hearty voice giving a cheeky glance towards her husband who by now was reluctantly beginning to see the funny side to it all.

"Hee hee, reckon you ought to be in the decorating business hubby with a style like this," she went on, reaching further up the wall with a damp cloth.

Berry made a boyish grin in response to her humour, feeling quite stupid about his actions. Little did he realise that his wife had cleverly seized the moment into cashing in on his temporary moment of embarrassment hoping in his weakness she might just begin to win a little sympathy for her *daft* ideas.

CHAPTER 10

THE LETTER

Clatter clomp! The familiar sound of the letterbox sent two sprawling boys skidding down the polished wooden floorboards to be first to seize the post – frequently a spot of breakfast time rivalry before school.

"Luther! Herbert! Stop that immediately!" shouted Ma. "If I've told you once I've told you a thousand times about that, you'll rip the letters."

"Aye up dad it's from t' 'ome office or summat, bet it's another hangin' job," shouted Luther.

Suddenly the whistling swoosh of Ma's wet dishcloth made a slapping connection with the back of Luther's head sending him neatly hurtling in the direction of a rather stern looking father.

"I'll take that lad ... and if I ever hear you talking like that again I'll tan yer hide. The fewer folk who know about my job the better – d' yer 'ear me?"

"S ... sorry dad ... they 'all know about it at school, well me friends an' all I mean ... they think yer a 'ero fer gettin' rid o' all them baddies."

"Do they now? Well tell them I'll be after them if they don't shut up about it," smirked father as he turned towards the kitchen, his fingers peeling open the envelope.

Hmm …! he murmured to himself, stroking his chin. "This one's different."

He scanned the letter with focussed concentration and continued to mumble some of its content to himself.

"What's that dearest? Can't hear what you're saying," said Sarah pushing away two cheeky eaves dropping boys eager to know who dad was hanging next.

"Aye get off to school sharp or I'll put me boot up yer backsides!" their father retorted.

Packing the two lads through the door the Berry's sat down aside the kitchen table and began peering at the official looking letter:-

ON HER MAJESTY'S SERVICE

HOME OFFICE

NORWICH CASTLE PRISON

NORWICH

HEREBY SUMMON THE APPOINTED DUTY OF EXCECUTIONER FOR THE ADMINISTRATION AND RESPONSIBILITY FORTHWITH:

R H Brassington

Mr James Berry of: Cliffe Road, Bradford.
Date, 16th November

It is the court's decision that on the sentencing for murder, an approved and professional person be sought for the correct and humane execution of one Mr Robert Goodale to be carried out at Norwich Castle on:

Monday November 30th at 8 o clock precisely.

The Home Office official representatives:
Mr Dent, Governor
Dr Stevenson
Dr Barr
Rev. Wheeler.
Mr Hales, Under-Sheriff

Mr Mason, High Sheriff of Norfolk.Hereby require you to attend an official preparatory meeting at H M P Norwich at 11-00 AM on Saturday the 28th of November, which will be chaired by Physician Dr Barr. Owing to certain matters pertaining to modern methods of Capital Punishment, it has been deemed necessary to make you aware of some changes that have come to our notice as a result of recent medical opinion. We therefore strongly recommend that you meet with us for discussion on the above date and time prior to any further administrations of Capital Punishment.

Please let me know if you would like us to make arrangements for your accommodation in advance.

We look forward to your prompt reply.
Yours sincerely,

Mr R H Mason.   High Sheriff.

"Hmmm ... sounds a bit urgent this one Ma, looks as if I'll have to get cracking an' reply today – so as they get the letter well before."

"We've plenty o' time love it's not until next weekend an' I'll get your best shirt an' collar ironed an' starched in the meantime ... gotta look yer best now," said Sarah.

"Aye … hmm ... *changes* eh? *That have come to our notice* ... hmm, I wonder what that's all about?"

Suddenly an unpleasant thought struck him:

"Damn! ... I bet it's all that Dr Barr's doin'! 'e's gotta interfere! .... I know… he'll be wantin' me to lengthen the drop – that's it. I've told him time and time again, I always stick to the guidelines laid down by Mr Marwood's table of drops and I've never had any trouble. It's too long … too long I keep telling him. One day you'll have me pullin' a blokes 'ead off!"

Berry was now pondering hard; stroking his chin in deep thought, and was almost on the edge of one of his melancholy dips when Sarah skilfully distracted him from his dive by sliding a nice hot mug of tea under his gaze plus a handsome slice of his favourite home baked cherry cake.

"There y' are pet get that down yer, then y' can sort that letter out after."

Berry's momentary gloom pleasantly gave way to a more cheerful smile as he responded to his wife's kind gesture.

It wasn't long before the following weekend arrived and James Berry was once again getting geared up for professional duties. His wife Sarah knew this only too well. He planned to take the early train on the Saturday morning from the Midland station, Bradford in order to arrive at Norwich in time to take a cab to where the meeting was to be held at the prison.

But as for Sarah those last few days leading up to husband's departure for duty were becoming a nightmare. Berry had started to form a dreadful habit since the business with John Lee and it looked doomed to get worse. Come evening or midday – sometimes both, he would often be found in the local pub flushing down the pints and finishing with a couple of cheap gins "for the road" as he put it.

Any normal man would know when to stop whenever finances or just uncontrolled behaviour signalled up, but not James Berry. As the fluid went down so his foul nature rose up only to reveal a part which poor

Sarah feared whenever he returned through the door after a session.

Berry had started on a long road to self-destruction. Normally, when at his best he could show a compassionate and even sensitive side to his nature, but things were beginning to change. It was obvious the job was beginning to take its toll and the soothing companionship of the *bottle* in preparation for the job in hand, may have started off as a good servant, but was going to end up as a bad master.

It was after one of his Friday afternoon sessions when the boisterous Berry came bounding through the door in his usual style. He was a large man but when on a full tank could give the illusion of being much larger – especially to a petite and defenceless woman desperately trying to keep him sweet.

"Izz me dinner ready woman … weer is it?" Berry slurred out his question which was more of a gruff command than a request.

"Right here pet ... all ready for you ... your favourite."

Sarah served out the stew and dumplings; just the right amount; right gravy and right temperature. She had learned from previous experience that to get any one thing wrong whenever he was in one of his booze moods could result in the dinner, plate and all being flung sideways.

"Have a nice time at the pub pet? ... Like some pudding in a bit .... err it's jam roly-poly, yer like that don't yer?"

"Ahh goo on then lass ... meck sure it's 'ot ... can't stand cold custud ...'specially when a 've 'ad sum ale."

Sarah skilfully ministered to the whimsical husband whilst at the same time keeping a tightrope balance on the conversation, hoping to gradually steer him towards an afternoon nap which often aided his recovery from a potentially volatile state.
Eventually the inebriated man rose from the dining table accompanied by a loud but satisfied belch, and wobbled his way towards the couch in the adjacent room; nicely prepared for in advance by a perceptive wife.

As the afternoon wore on things got generally calmer especially as by now the "lion" was sleeping. Meanwhile out in the back yard Luther and Herbert were kicking a ball around; bouncing and heading to and fro to each other knowing it was better to pass the time outdoors when Dad had been to the pub.

Suddenly, without warning, half a brick whistling airborne between the two of them crashed violently with a resounding "dong!" into a tin bath tub hanging on the outside kitchen wall. Luckily, a matter of about a couple of feet to one side would have nicely seen off the kitchen window.

The wall height plus the trajectory of the missile placed the origin of this dastardly act squarely in the alley-way which ran next to the Berry's garden. Luther and Herbert were on it like a shot. Now nearing their early teens, they were able to scale the high wall with nimble ease to find two local rivals scurrying round the alley end into a jitty leading to the allotments.

"C'mon Lu, I know where they've gone. Let's sneak round the back o' t' factory an' surprise 'em eh?"

"Ahh good un Herb, giz that stick theer ... I'll give 'em a reyt good beatin'."

The lads tore off in hot pursuit and were gone for the rest of the afternoon, which also meant that they were well out of the way when Dad stirred from his slumber. Diplomacy was crucial and required a fair amount of Sarah's skill if James was to arise pleasantly. Usually a mug of tea did the trick and Sarah would keep the kettle simmering next to the fire range in readiness, constantly looking for signs of his stirring.

The day was gently heading towards evening and Sarah was enjoying a peaceful hour's knitting. She had almost forgotten about the boys outside when it suddenly dawned on her that all was quiet in the back yard – in fact it had been so for at least an hour. Of course being pre-occupied with her husband's antics she had completely missed the fact that they had been home from school ages and not had anything to eat. Startled by her own thoughts she involuntarily jumped up to check outside, knocking a half empty cold mug of tea into the gaping visage of the sleeping man. To attempt to describe his vocal response would be beyond polite words.

One could normally chuckle at a scene like this, seeing the man jerk and splutter in the manner of an upturned turtle, but not this time. Berry could be quite nasty when enraged, particularly in an environment where he didn't have to be on his best behaviour. The "Lord of the Manor", the "King of the Castle" had been humiliated in his own home, and that subconsciously gave him licence to act as he felt fit. Sarah picked up a nearby tea towel hoping to reverse the mistake, if that were possible, but she knew it was too late. Instead, gripped by fear she froze to the spot clasping the cloth tightly against her chest – eyes wide like a frightened rabbit in a searchlight, waiting for what was to happen next.

Meanwhile, realising they had nipped off without telling anyone – and worse completely missed teatime, the boys were frantically dashing back home.

"Sorry Mum ... sorry Dad ... didn't know what time it wor," Luther gasped, hardly able to get his breath as they both burst through the door.

If ever they had picked a bad time to come home late then this was one of those.

"Time?... time! ... I'll give yer time damn you! ... boots off an' upstairs now!" boomed the angry master.

Fortunately for Sarah the timing of the boy's arrival had conveniently diverted her husband's fire; the boys however were not going to be so lucky – Berry was already beginning to un-buckle his belt.

CHAPTER 11

BOWLAND STREET MISSION

"For Thine is the kingdom the power and the glory forever and ever amen" – droned the routine mumblings of the pious Berry's final rounding of the Lord's Prayer, and with it a signal to Sarah, eavesdropping in the hallway, to serve up a hearty bacon and egg breakfast for the man with a mission. When about to embark on professional duties Berry would rise early, wash, dress and then shut himself in a spare room known as his museum; aptly named owing to his small collection of memoirs and artefacts from previous hangings which he had found useful when giving his lectures. This spare room was also devoted to his official duties where he could gather his thoughts including saying a short prayer in preparation for the day ahead. Sarah had it in mind to give him a good send off knowing he would probably be gone well into the next week, which would give her opportunity to sneak off to Bowland Street Mission on the Sunday morning whilst he was away.

For a long time now Sarah had a mind to one day satisfy her curiosity about all the rumours she had heard concerning the Mission, and with husband James being off for the weekend on duties it was too good an opportunity not to miss.

It was just after 10 o'clock on the Sunday morning, the boys were happily occupied playing round at one of their friends, when Sarah gingerly stepped through the mission door. She decided to arrive late purposely so as to be unnoticed, as her intention was not to get too involved for fear of being found out by her husband, who of course did not approve. Also the congregation would be in full swing, heartily praising the lord – happily clapping away an' all, so probably wouldn't give her much attention. The church being usually full meant she would be able to dilute herself more easily.

Bowland Street Mission was one on its own. A new breed of evangelical revivalists of that ol' time religion was sweeping the land, and the upsurge of the Old Gospel at Bowland Street was no exception. History has shown that Christian revivalists have often been viewed with some kind of scepticism at first during their early pioneer days, only to be hailed by later historians with honour and praise. This was new; a re-awakening that was attracting more and more folk away from the traditional establishment. It appealed to all, irrespective of class, creed, colour or background – a fraternity who had one thing in common and that was to see the power of the gospel change lives. Quite often Bowland Street Mission would have to have several meetings on a Sunday in good order to accommodate the demands of eager worshippers. And each time the building would be full to capacity. So what was it that inspired such enthusiasm and following? Often lively music and joyful praise could be heard outside cheerfully touching the hearts of passers-by; shamelessly letting the world know that this happy euphoric throng had found relevance and reality in their new found faith.

"What a friend we have in Jesus ..." would be one of the many hymns, or rather songs – sung with gusto, swinging along to a happy-clappy jangle of piano and tambourine – totally different from any church going ritual which some were used to. Yet in contrast, any hysterical frenzied whip-up was out of the question. Often the meeting would be led in silence or even within the normality of children chirping and laughing, as they do, only to be suddenly aware of yet another wave of the move of the Holy Spirit embracing the congregation and leading the meeting.

These folk saw the church as the people; the building was secondary and there was a spirit of genuineness and compassion here especially towards those in need. The other attractive thing was its leader; none other than Smith Wigglesworth who drew crowds like a magnet. A Bradford plumber who came to faith at 8 years old (saved, born again – call it what you may) later taught to read and write by his wife Polly, became a world class evangelist bringing revival to the nation and wherever else he was sent throughout the world. Wow! When you walked into Bowland St. mission you came into God's presence. It was even known for drunks and raucous layabouts to drift in off the street only to be suddenly sobered up on contact with the Holy presence. This was Bowland Street, to where Mrs Berry would later sneak off whenever she could.

The air was electric. Sarah had never encountered a church like this before. The first thing that struck her was a large quotation, presumably from the Bible, in large letters on the wall behind the platform pulpit which read: "I AM THE LORD THAT HEALETH THEE". It was obvious that this was quite central to their faith; evident by the many testimonies to healing miracles which she'd heard from local gossip.

Gradually the congregation calmed down and a more meditative atmosphere developed which seemed to last for several minutes as if people were waiting for something to happen. Sarah eagerly watched, eyes partly closed so as to appear praying but open enough to peep. Then things began to stir. Quite out of the blue a young woman began singing, totally unaccompanied, yet with a voice so beautiful it tingled the very soul. Hardly able to keep still, Sarah suddenly found herself humming along to the tune herself being totally absorbed in the spirit of the moment. Slowly others were beginning to catch on as well, fusing into a corporate harmony akin to nothing short of a Heavenly choir. *How different,* she thought, this had all come about spontaneous, un-rehearsed yet perfect. But then just as this happened something else followed: Almost unnoticed, Sarah realised that the congregation had settled down into a quiet background tone and the girl was singing in an entirely different language – incomprehensible but speaking so eloquently to the soul that the actual meaning of words didn't matter. How calming and relaxing, she had not felt this peaceful for ages.

Eventually the young woman finished her song and folks sat down in focussed anticipation of what was to come next. A smartly dressed, middle aged gentleman stepped up to the platform and placed a large partly opened Bible on the lectern. Everyone knew that Mr Wigglesworth was about to deliver his sermon.

This preacher never minced his words – always "taking the bull by the horns" as the saying goes. Frequently opening up with a good quote from his "sword", meaning his Bible, he would set the scene.

Just about to lunge forth, finger poised trigger-like on an appropriate passage in his large preacher's Bible, Wigglesworth suddenly paused as if something had quickened him from within. Grabbing a nearby hymn-book he calmly found the page he was looking for, took a deep breath and started to sing out a verse from a famous Wesleyan hymn, ringing to the rafters in good old Yorkshire style:

"His blood can ma … ke the foul-est clean … his blood avails for me … His blood avails for me …"

And so he went on; accompanied by a few folk near the front in full agreement with the powerful significance of this message, eventually coming to an end after a few minutes.

After a short pause and re-gaining his thoughts Wigglesworth began to speak:

"I believe the Lord wishes me to speak on this message today and not the one I prepared … God's love can reach the vilest of men! I said God's love can reach the vilest – the vilest of men!" he said repeatedly pressing down his large hand on the Bible indicating firm faith in what he had just proclaimed.

"It doesn't matter who you are or what you've done, the Bible says we have all fallen short of the Glory of God – not one of us deserves a place in Heaven – we're all sinners, none of us is good enough and that's it!" But the good news is we can be made good enough through the atoning blood of Jesus who died in your place on the cross – who took our punishment … all we have to do is accept it ... accept the miracle of new birth through Jesus … it's a gift! ... so what's so difficult about that?"

The words hit Sarah like a thunderbolt. Her thoughts went immediately to her husband whom she knew had been having an inward battle for some time now concerning the type of work he did.

Oh God, she thought to herself. *If only … if only that could be.*

"It's no good saying – oh well I've never done anyone any harm I've always tried to be good – hey who are yer comparin' yerself with to finish up with that idea? Who are you to judge who's good or bad? We're all on the same level with this! Sin is sin! Rotten is rotten, corruption's corruption and death's death, it's as simple as that. There's no half sins no bits of sins it's all the same in God's eyes … Eternity's a dangerous place to muck about with – I say eternity's a dangerous place … we're all heading there … make sure you're not there on your own! That's why we need a friend – a saviour! – get it?"

Pentecostal preachers in those days were not exactly noted for their short sermons; when the Spirit moved you could expect to be in for a long haul. Smith Wigglesworth had been in full flow now for a good forty minutes or so and folks were, as usual, soaking up every word. The mission however was missing one vital piece of equipment, normally an important part of any place of public gathering – namely a clock. Time wasn't important when preaching the gospel – it had full priority and saving souls from a lost eternity was the mission statement. Mr Wigglesworth continued for a while longer and his message was becoming more clear and relevant to Sarah as the minutes ticked by. The meeting eventually came to a close with another rousing Wesleyan hymn and Sarah looked round hoping to find a means of finding out the time.

Just then a lady caught her attention.

"Good morning sister, nice to see you here … enjoy the meeting?" said the rather kind looking lady.

"Err … yes … yes … I did thank you, it was very good," she replied.

"Well you're always welcome here any time and if we can help with anything at all – well my name's Polly… Smith's wife … it's nice to meet you."

"Thank you … I'm Sarah. Yes it was a lovely meeting, shame it was so short, I could have listened to your husband all day."

"Short … short did you say? Goodness me sister it's half-past twelve we've been here two and a half hours you must have really enjoyed it."

Sarah had been so lost in the spirit that the whole meeting seemed to have passed in a moment giving her the feeling that she had only just walked through the door and been greeted by the kind lady.

Something had happened – definitely happened to Sarah in that building and she was only just beginning to realise it.

"Well I must go now Mrs Wigglesworth – err Polly, thank you so much … I have to collect the boys."

"Of course … but it is good to meet you Sarah – here take this little gift, keep it – it's a little New Testament, don't like our visitors to leave empty handed."

"Well thank you Polly, that's very kind."

"That's fine love … see you again probably … bye," said Polly giving her a warm handshake and quick peck on the cheek.

Walking out of the Mission building things seemed different. Instead of seeing the grimy industrialised Bradford buildings and scruffy alleyways she found herself drawn to focus on the green trees in the park. She had never noticed before how green and beautiful things could really look, and yet she had lived in the neighbourhood all her life. Now the world looked different – brighter, cleaner, as if the summer season had just returned for her alone. Trees and grass looked greener; the air felt soft and smelled sweet yet it was Autumn. How strange, before everything had looked drab and murky. Her whole perception had been altered –seeing the world through a new pair of lenses, everything about Creation was vibrant and purposeful, and she was part of it. What the preacher said was true – new birth! Yes that was it! … new birth … new vision and in such a simple way she had received that very gift.

She made haste to collect the boys, finding a new spring in her heels as if walking on air.

CHAPTER 12

THE NORWICH MESS

For the next few days Sarah was on cloud nine. Cheerfully going about daily chores; seeing the kids off to school each morning with a kiss and encouraging smile for the day, and generally feeling good to be alive. Husband James had of course been on extended duties during this time and was not expected to get home until Tuesday evening. However it was now Thursday and there was no sign of James nor was there any message from the Home Office explaining any delay he might have incurred as a result of extra demands on his appointment. By now of course everything should have been over and done with as far as the execution itself was concerned, which had been set to take place on the Monday morning of the same week.

Of course, by now there's bound to be something in the papers about it ... best get a newspaper, she thought. *Perhaps there'll be some clue there, they usually mention when a criminal has been administered justice - even if it's only brief.*

Meanwhile James Berry was not having a good time at all. His worst fears about the outcome of the meeting had been realised. A heated row had blown up over the medical science and the length of drop, against Berry's professional judgement which of course was based on his approved and efficient finely-tuned Marlow method. But the weight of the establishment was against him, after all he was only a hangman who did the dirty part of the job – they were the real professionals, the medics, the ones who had that special mystique which naturally put them on the high ground. In the end Berry was forced to compromise after Dr Barr snidely suggested that if Berry wished to continue in the profession with their support – which everyone knew he couldn't practise without – then he would have to move with the times. Berry was incensed. Rising sharply to his feet, flipping his chair violently over with his large backside Berry retorted:

"Well damn the lot of you then! If it takes blackmail to cunningly prise me out of my position Barr, maybe you ought to be pulling the damn lever yourself on Monday an' not me! ... But just remember this all of yer, if it goes wrong – on your head be it!"

Berry continued for a few moments longer; red faced and wagging his finger at the startled committee. Eventually after Berry's anger was spent, the undersheriff cleared his throat and nervously fumbling his pocket watch, suggested they all adjourn for an early lunch and a spot of fresh air, thus giving breathing space and diffusing the tension for all concerned.

Peering into the front page of the daily newspaper the headline was plain enough:

GOODALE HANGED AT NORWICH FOR WIFE MURDER

Sarah quickly scanned through the details pertaining to her husband's involvement with the report hoping to spot any clue for his delay. Picking up on the last few lines of the column, it was beginning to make horrible sense:

... although the execution was fully in compliance with Home Office guidelines, certain complications which happened at the time of death have deemed it necessary to warrant further investigation as part of a full inquest.

It was becoming plain to Sarah that all had not gone to plan and there was more to it than what the newspapers were permitted to say.

Why would they put this on the front page? she thought. *And with just a scanty outline report in a short column - the sort of thing you might normally find mid page.*

It was becoming more and more obvious that some kind of deal had been struck with the papers: a sort of *well you can put it front page but limit the details till after the inquest*, type deal – in other words a cover up.

Feeling somewhat bewildered Sarah steadily made her way home passing the park and hoping to spot the boys.

It was the following day when Berry finally arrived home. He had not had an easy journey either. Constantly aware that it was only a matter of time before the full details of the Norwich mess hit the news stand, he was becoming increasingly paranoid that people were avoiding him; recognising who he was. Maybe this was the reason why he sat alone in the train compartment because no-one else would sit near him, he thought. It was of course absurd to think that – not everyone knew what this famous hangman looked like – at least not yet.

The state of depression was something that Berry was finding increasingly easy to slip into. Reaching into his pocket he pulled out his comforter; his hip flask which was becoming a regular habit by now in order to anaesthetise any mental pain. His train was about half an hour away from Bradford when suddenly the whole carriage went dark and smoke filled the compartment.

"Aggh! Oh God save me. Don't send me there don't send me there!"

Not fully realising, on approach to Bradford the train had entered the darkness of the Clayton tunnel with the compartment window open, explaining the appearance of smoke from the locomotive; Berry thought he had gone to Hell. Being so preoccupied with self-pity he had not only forgotten to close the compartment window in case of smoke but had completely sunk into a gloomy abyss. The experience at Norwich had almost sent him over the top and was the start of a condition which was to get worse.

In his stupor Berry had placed himself back on the Norwich Castle gallows again pulling the lever. He watched Goodale disappear down the hole. Suddenly the rope jerked then flirted back up again as if it had snapped. Then, horror! And his worst fears … Peering down the trap lay the grotesque sight of a decapitated body.

"Oh my Lord!" he screamed, "I tried … Lord I tried to tell them the rope was too long but they wouldn't listen … wouldn't listen!"

Suddenly with a thunderous roar the train burst out of the tunnel into bright sunlight, and with it Berry who was able to snap himself back to reality.

It took him several minutes to recover from his ghoulish trance, and with the sunlight and fresh air now pouring through the window it enabled him to clear his thoughts.

Well I suppose it was their responsibility, after all they did overrule my advice … told them so – told them.

By this time he had fiddled out a letter from within his inside pocket and was peering over some reassuring lines on the page.

It read that after a brief inquest following the trying ordeal the Governor and Gaol Surgeon had given supporting evidence as to the care with which every detail had been carried out and that no blame would be placed on the hangman or anyone else who carried out their duties within the Law. *Hmm … well I suppose that's fine for them! They have to stick together I suppose, or else if one goes down the lot go down an' all … huh!*

… But it doesn't work like that, they'll all find friends in high places to nicely put them in a good light, leaving me in the shade … folks 'll still blame the hangman for a botched job.

The train pulled into Bradford station and Berry headed for home. He decided to skip the cab this time and walk the couple of miles instead – via the pub.

Meanwhile Sarah, who still had no idea when her husband would arrive, had already got a few things in readiness for when he might walk through the door. She was getting quite used to this by now. James's unpredictable behaviour on arrival demanded certain skills from his wife in order not to create a scene. Some of the neighbours had already moved due to the many rows that emanated from inside the house, not to mention the odd neighbourly skirmish outside.

It was becoming blatantly obvious that life could not go on in this way for much longer – something had to be done – but what? This was the inner cry from Sarah and if truth be known from her husband as well.

It was late in the evening when her husband finally arrived and Sarah was curled up in front of the fire reading her little New Testament Bible given to her by Polly Wigglesworth. She had been able to gain some inner strength from the comfort of its pages from time to time. Finally Berry arrived home and as expected a little worse for wear. Sarah quickly rose to her feet, and habitually patting her apron straight she inadvertently flipped the New Testament onto the floor, landing it directly in the path of the meandering husband. She had been trying to keep its existence secret, knowing that he might ask too many questions which could lead to his finding out where she had got it from. She had to think quickly.

"Oh lovely to see you pet," smiling and walking towards him, skilfully nudging the Bible under the table with her foot.

"Did it all go well – no problems I mean?"

James never made a sound except for a nod and a gruff "Huh!" in response. Swerving to one side, avoiding any welcoming contact with his wife, he headed straight for the stairs and to bed, seemingly totally oblivious to the small Bible falling to the floor.

Sarah stood almost motionless for a while; quite taken aback by her husband's quirky manner on arrival – nothing new of course as this was rapidly becoming the norm, especially after he'd been to the pub.

Ah well, she thought … *might as well continue reading … now then where did it go I wonder?*

Waiting until her husband was out of the way, Sarah picked up the Bible from under the table, where she'd flicked it with her foot; curled back into her fireside chair and began thumbing the pages. Suddenly her eyes fixed their gaze on three hand written words on the blank side of the publisher's verso page near the front. She had probably skimmed past this many times before without even noticing it.

How strange, I'm sure it wasn't there before ... I would have noticed it.

But there it was, neatly penned with great care and presentation:

Prayer changes things

Normally she might have nonchalantly skipped over this with an unconscious glance whilst flipping the pages towards the scriptures. But now it seemed, the words had not only got her attention but were having quite an impact.

Without hesitation Sarah found herself surprisingly half kneeling already as if by an involuntary response; perched on the floor and turned to rest her elbows on the seat – hands prayerfully clasped. It was no co-incidence that the words should appear to her now whereas previously they had been unnoticed, and at just the right time when things were sinking to such a low ebb.

"Oh God … help him! … Oh God help us all!" she tearfully stammered out the muffled groan – nothing pious or religious, her plight was beyond all that.

"Oh God if you're really up there just do something … anything! I can't go on with this man much longer."

Emotionally exhausted, Sarah lay crouched with her head resting on the chair cushion and would have almost fallen asleep if it hadn't been for the hall clock chiming the midnight hour. Reluctantly, after tidying a few things she decided it would be better to sleep downstairs and make herself more comfortable on the large chair, believing that James would be fast asleep by now, and would not wish to be disturbed.

CHAPTER 13

NICE ONE BERRY

The following day's atmosphere was to say the least somewhat heavy. A particular gloom rested on the Berry household which seemed to affect all within. Trying desperately to hold the bare threads of family spirit together Sarah cautiously attended to her early morning domestic duties in necessary preparation for the day ahead. Barely sleeping a wink during the night, which she had spent curled up on the large chair, Sarah had devotedly risen early and was already preparing the children's breakfast when Luther burst into the kitchen.

"Hey up mam … what's up wi me fatha … 'e's makin' a reight funny noise as if 'e's drownin' or summat?... Ah think 'e's deed!"

"Oh my Lord," exclaimed Sarah.

Dropping everything she swiftly scurried up the stairs only to find her husband hanging semi prone out of bed, looking quite blue and desperately gagging for air. The fool in his over indulgence of alcohol the day before was choking on his own vomit. Sarah angrily reminded him of this as she franticly turned him to the floor whacking his back to clear an airway, but also venting her anger for his stupidity.

"Is he orreight mam?" shouted Luther from the bottom of the stairs.

By now the *casualty of drink* had got the entire attention of the family as they all gathered into the bedroom to witness the drama.

"Aye he's alright lads … he's just got a touch of *bottle sickness* after a session at t' ale house. Take a good look lads, this is what ale can do … just make sure you don't finish up like him!"

Luther and Herbert gazed, wide eyed at the pathetic heap on the floor covered in vomit – this was their father whom they were supposed to look up to.

"Not a very good example is it lads?" Sarah went on.

"Now get yerselves ready fer school an' be off wi' yer!"

Not needing telling twice, the lads quickly shot down the stairs in response – hardly wanting to spend another minute in the putrid air of their father's bedroom.

Gradually after several glasses of water and a thorough clean up Berry came to his senses. Sarah changed the bed sheets and then thought it best to attend to the needs of her husband. But no sooner had he recovered from his ordeal than he was out; making the excuse that he'd some important business to attend to. Of course Sarah knew only too well that the only business he had would eventually direct him to the pub as soon as it was opening time.

He's not going to change, she thought.

" 'As a dog returns to his vomit so a fool returns to his folly' – goes the proverb. Aye that's my Jim alright," she muttered.

Surprisingly the rest of the day seemed to pass with relative ease for Sarah; attending to the day's domestic demands helped take her mind off the morning's chaotic start. And so the day came and went without much of a hitch. Even the later arrival of James from his "official duties" went quite uncannily smoothly, considering some of his antics demonstrated many times in the past. And so the months passed.

One Saturday morning seemed to bring with it a wind of change as the Master of the household stood pleasantly smiling in the kitchen doorway.

"What a beautiful day it is today lads! … is there any football on in t' park this afternoon?"

Somewhat taken aback by the surprise of their father's attitude and his suitable readiness for any outdoor activity he could accompany the boys with, the lads were momentarily speechless.

"… err ah … I mean yes dad – i'nt that reight Luther?" stammered Herbert in response.

Peering up from the breakfast table Luther couldn't help spluttering the words over his mug of tea in enthusiastic response.

"… Yeh … Herb … an' I'm play … p … playin' centre forward an' all."

"Ah yer cumin' to watch us Dad?" chimed in Herbert.

"Aye … I thought I might nip down this aft' an' give you lads a bit of a cheer an' all, yer know."

"Kick off about two o' clock is it lads?"

Yeh dad … yeh … that's it."

"Alright, I'll 'ave a walk down with you in plenty of time then."

116

"Wow! Great dad – c'mon Luth' let's get us boots dubbed up ready," said Herbert, eagerly shoving his brother almost off his stool towards the door.

Meanwhile Sarah had been eavesdropping on the entire conversation from the other room and was determined to keep well out of the way so as not to spoil the momentum of the plan.

Trying desperately to keep a cheerful expression from giving the show away she eventually entered the kitchen, and pretending to act as if she knew nothing, gingerly greeted her husband.

"Morning love! Nice day isn't it? Have you much to do?"

"Aye … thought I might pop down to t' park an' give the lads a bit of a cheer on at t' football match they've got goin' with their friends … yer know - like."

"Oo … that 'll be good." she replied acting surprised. "Do yer want me to do you a couple o' sandwiches or summat love?"

"… err … aye … goo on then lass … yer can come an' all if yer want – mind you yer probably too busy wi 'things."

Sarah was flabbergasted, but daren't show it.

What's this? she thought. *My goodness ... bit of an answer t' prayer this one Lord ... huh! I'll believe it if it lasts ... nah! ... He'll just be feelin' guilty – an so he should!*

"… err right then … I'll make us up a bottle o' lemonade an' all – should be real nice day."

The afternoon arrived and Luther and Herbert set off with their dad towards the park. Sarah had decided to stay behind for a while, giving herself more time to get a picnic basket together – football after all was a man's sport so to turn up about half time with refreshments seemed more appropriate.

The game was going well and by half time the lad's team were up two goals to one. When Sarah eventually arrived there was a good spirit in the air plus a few smiling faces; something which was indeed welcome, and hopefully might even be a much needed turning point in the Berry household. This was nice; for a few quality moments the Berry's sat together on the grass round the brown paper picnic tablecloth, enjoying a spot of early spring sunshine. After a while the boys began fidgeting as their thoughts were starting to focus on the second half of the match.

"Goo on then lads … give em what for," nodded their dad approvingly.

By now the Referee – another one of the parents – was positioning himself near the centre for the kick-off; a sharp blast on the whistle and the game was soon under way.

No sooner the kick-off than the Berry lads, now with newly inspired morale due to the presence of their parents, eagerly took possession of the ball. The whack of dubbin soaked leather boots on case-ball; the highly testosterone charged youthy grunts and shouts from these energetic sportsmen was drawing fierce competition from the opposing forward line – the battle was on! Woof! Wallow! – woof! pounded the banter and volley as players won, lost, passed and tackled; slid, grappled and tugged in pursuit of the much desired bag of wind.

"Pressure! – pressure! Keep on at em lads" roared a voice.

"Don't let 'em rob thee!" bawled another.

"Goo on Berry! Goo on! Tha nearly theer lad … now … belt it! Belt it!"

Young Luther was in prime position now with only a last defender between him and the goal keeper, with seconds gone and no time for even the quickest decision, impulse was the only thing left; the young Berry booted the ball with every ounce of punch he'd got left – Woolf! ... back of the net! What a spectacle! What a goal, but what a disaster. The young Berry had booted the ball with so much force that the leather stitching holding the leather ball's casing together had completely ripped apart, leaving the bladder to part company with its outer skin. In short the bladder went wildly off in one direction whilst the casing went on to score the goal. The crowd were hysterical; several of the spectators fell about laughing whilst the ref. shook his head in sheer disbelief.

"Nice one Berry – nice one!" came a guttural shout from one of the spectators.

But any victorious cheers were soon dashed by the referee as he stood there shaking his head and wagging his finger in disapproval – "No, no- no! ... can't have that – disallowed."

 Fierce shrieks and hollering from supporters on both sides sounded like things might get out of hand if the ref didn't do something quickly to appease the crowd. The bit that looked like a ball had indeed gone into the net yet the other bit that made it a ball, and gave it its soul, hadn't. Was it a goal or not? Is half a ball half a goal? "Ridiculous!" This of course was what the ranting was all about. Almost bursting a blood vessel out of sheer desperation, the ref gave a couple of long blasts on his whistle; momentarily gaining a sufficient gap in the uproar to be able to announce his decision.

"Free kick - free kick!" The ref firmly pointed to a spot on the edge of what was probably the penalty area, allowing them another direct shot if they wished to take it. A few obvious murmurings emitted from one or two participants in expected disagreement, but then after all most realised that it was fair. The only problem of course now was – the ball.

"All right you lot!" bawled the ref. "If you don't find a ball soon you don't get a match … shake yerselves, 'cos I'm not standin' 'ere all day."

It wasn't long before one of the lads found a suitable replacement amongst some of the kit at the other end of the field and proudly booted it towards the ref.

"Will that do ref? it's a bit tatty … one we sometimes have a bit of a kick-around with, but it's reight an' all."

The ball whistled its way over and landed itself somewhere near the ref, enabling him to neatly flip it up with his foot and catch it; of course but only after giving it a couple of header nods so as to show off his prowess to the crowd. On inspection of the ball the ref looked a little puzzled.

"Hey - up! What's this?"

The ref was squinting his eyes at a crudely white painted face, plus the name BOB, on the casing of the ball. Some of the lads started to giggle others looked more sheepish as if someone might have to explain.

"Hee – hee, go on lads put me outa me misery … I'm dyin' t' know … who is he?"

After a brief silence one of the more extravert members of the teams grinningly piped up.

"… err … it's … it's that theer bloke who got dun fer murderin' 'is wife … a bloke called Goodale or summat."

He was of course referring to Robert Goodale who the newspapers had said was hanged for the murder, but of course the lads, at this stage, were probably not yet up to date with any details.

"Ahh … hee - hee … we thought we might just kick 'is 'ead around for a bit, being he was a bad bloke an' all that," chimed in another one of the lads hardly being able to hold himself up for laughing.

On hearing this James Berry was horrified!

How much did they know? he thought. *How long would it take before the public got to know about the horrible mess at Norwich?*

How uncanny was this? They were, although in their innocence, symbolically kicking around Goodale's head unbeknown to everyone there. But who might know? And of course who knew that this was one monumentous issue in Berry's life.

Berry was feeling very uneasy. Glances were being cast towards him now from folks around. Of course some already knew the nature of his job and could have been aware of the latest events. He was rapidly beginning to feel himself caving in to the pressure which might manifest itself in some form of volatile outburst. But just as the embarrassment was about to crush Berry the ref gave a sharp blast on his whistle, timely replacing everyone's attention back on the game. The welcomed relief from the ordeal was a nice time for him to take advantage of the gap of opportunity, and to slip away just as the crowd were heartily cheering the successful scoring of a well-deserved goal.

It had become pretty obvious to Sarah that something had seriously disturbed her husband she thought it best to leave him to simmer for a while in his own way, and catch up with him later when the match was over.

CHAPTER 14

A BLEAK FUTURE

Time had passed since the Norwich mess but unfortunately for Berry the whole business had taken its toll. As he feared, the sordid event eventually leaked through the media; sifting its way onto the *jungle telegraph* and making meaty local gossip, lasting well into the following year before its fascination finally yielded to a newer topic. Uneasy times were ahead for this lonely man. He had felt the gradual pressure of change creeping on him for a while now, and was finding it difficult to accept. The whole business of the death penalty was macabre enough, not to mention the role of the executioner, and none of this was helped by gnawing pressure from a growing minority of abolitionists. There was also a new feeling afoot that better judgement was needed in the courtroom, together with the reform of alternative methods of punishment for crimes of passion, and that circumstantial evidence alone could not always be relied upon to convict a person to death. The hay-day – if such a career could ever have such a thing as a hay-day, was no longer becoming as lucrative as it had been previously. The formal requests for his services were becoming less frequent: requests which in the past had been almost on a regular basis, despite the fact that he was always at the ready to travel anywhere in the United Kingdom, including Ireland or beyond. His health, or rather his mental state was getting worse, and his bank balance was suffering too. The future was not looking good. As for Sarah: she had just about given up; given up on any hope, faith and most of all given up on Berry. The poor woman had passed caring, and since her husband found out about her sneaky visits to Bowland Street Mission and that "damn plumber", he had subsequently banned her – any glimmer of Divine help seemed as far away as it could ever be.

One day Berry decided he'd had enough, and took leave of absence. Gaining some support from his physician decided to go away for a while to help his cause, hoping it might restore some normality to his miserable existence. He had persistently told the physician that he had developed certain chronic breathing difficulties which were probably exacerbated by a stressful job and consequent nervous condition. And after some irritating drama Berry had managed to persuade the physician enough to land himself a couple of weeks respite at a convalescent home near the sea.

During his time of escape he had managed to reflect on the whole business; hoping for a glimmer of something which might be his salvation from all this mess. So far he'd carried out 131 hangings within seven years of duties, including five women, some of whom may have been innocent, and now he was about to resign – the entire sordid affair of having to *kill people for a living* was abhorrent to say the least.

There has to be a better way to earn money, he thought.

Even when giving his lectures whilst on tour as a professional executioner he found himself supporting the abolition of the death penalty instead of promoting it. On the outside all looked successful and had indeed, during his seven or eight years in office, brought him substantial income and a comfortable lifestyle. But on the inside he was wracked with guilt and riddled with remorse and had become a despicable man with no peace in his soul. Again and again recurring powerful thoughts, visions and nightmares constantly bedevilled him, showing that capital punishment was wrong – so wrong! One hundred and thirty one times had he had the power of life or death over a person's fate, being the man who pulled the lever – this was too much for anyone to bear. There was nothing – nothing he could do to put the clock back or change history – what was done is done and could not be un-done. The die was cast and James Berry had to live or die with it.

If his fortnight's respite had been any help to him it at least gave him the chance to think alone and take the occasional stroll in the fresh sea air without anyone recognising or pestering him. But it would soon be over having served its purposeful time, and he would have to return to his grimy life, like one slipping into an old worn out, well-fitting coat, which is useless to be of any benefit. Berry was in a rut: wherever he went; whatever he did it would always hang over him that James Berry is, was and always will be – *an executioner,* which by his own admission meant that he was no better than any other murderer that he'd sent to eternity.

One night near the end of his stay there was a horrific storm: peals of thunder and flashes of lightning woke the entire convalescent home. The heavy wooden shutters which were closed for the first time in years rattled and banged trying to protect windows from flying branches and debris. According to staff it was one of the worst storms they'd seen for a long time and hoped and prayed that there was no small fishing craft caught out at sea that terrible night. The storm raged on for several hours. Buffeting tempestuous gusts showed no sign of relenting, until the early hours of the morning when the storm finally began to subside giving all within welcomed relief and some chance to catch up on lost sleep.

The following morning brought much calmer weather plus the occasional spot of sun peeping through the early morning clouds. Gradually some inmates and staff took a stroll round the Home's grounds and gardens, picking up debris and helping put things in their proper places. Later on Berry decided to wander off towards the cliff top hoping to catch a breath of fresh air before his departure in the early afternoon. Walking towards the cliff edge he suddenly became aware of groups of people frantically heading towards the same view point in anticipation of what they might see.

At the foot of the cliff, strewn along the rocks and shingles was the obvious wreck of a storm torn fishing vessel. Its hull and deck twisted with sharp broken planks; its sides burst open spilling fish and equipment over the entire area and the absence of its masts all suggested the boat had at some point lost control and had become entirely at the mercy of an angry storm. The place was buzzing with police, maritime officials and medical people searching through the wreckage and all along the shoreline looking for signs of life. Reports had come in that the Scarborough lifeboat had put out to sea during the night and had not returned. The boat and all 8 crew were missing!

How can men give their lives and voluntarily at that, to bravely risk all to save others? thought Berry.

It wasn't until later that news came through that the lifeboat had in fact beached further down the coast and had miraculously managed to rescue the entire crew of the stricken fishing boat ... but sadly not without cost. During the chaos one of the lifeboat crew, a seventeen year old boy, had been washed overboard and there seemed little hope of finding him alive.

When Berry heard this he was mortified. The thought of those brave men: sons, fathers, brothers an' all risking their lives in such impossible conditions all for someone they had probably never even met. But that was their lot, their calling their duty to fellow mankind, and to top it all a young man of seventeen years – a mere lad, to become a sacrifice to such a selfless cause – what a waste! How could he, a hangman, compare with this? How had he earned the right to be such a miserable excuse for a human being whose time on Earth had been spent taking life when this lad's short span had been spent trying to save it.

It wasn't right; there was no justice; it was unfair; life was unfair – he was unfair. Somehow there had to be some atonement for all the wickedness, unfairness and wrong that we are all inherently part of – something or someone either in this world or the next had to redress the balance.

Soon after lunch Berry packed a few things together and headed for the station in order to catch the train back to Bradford. Over the years he had travelled quite a lot on Britain's railway system and knew only too well the route his journey would take him to the Midland station at Bradford. The journey over the moors and countryside would normally be pleasant. But the one part he always dreaded was the last part of the voyage nearing Bradford when the train had to pass through Clayton Tunnel. There were two tunnels close together between Bradford and Halifax: the Queensbury and the Clayton; either one was bad enough for Berry – he hated tunnels. But the Clayton Tunnel had a reputation in the past for bad luck which naturally fuelled spooky stories of one sort or another, and Berry was superstitious enough without them.

Apparently some years before during its construction, some workmen were tragically killed due to the incompetence of a drunk in charge of a winding winch, resulting in two men suffering horrific death by being mangled in the machinery. Since that time nothing ever seemed to go right and many a ghostly tale had only added to the eerie ambience of the place. Berry had already had one bad experience passing through the tunnel when he returned from that awful day in Norwich and was in no fit mental state to suffer another.

Being adequately replenished with Dutch courage from his hip flask he handed himself a good extra nip in readiness.

On entering the tunnel it was if someone had thrown a switch – as if the very phantoms he feared knew he was coming. The roaring plunge of the train into the darkness of the Clayton tunnel triggered flashing vivid images on the screen of his mind. Faces, scenes and indelible memories etched themselves into his brain with such fury that he felt his head would burst. There was no relief from his tormenting demons; crushing guilt enveloped him with the strength of a python. Had it not been for the sudden burst of daylight at tunnel's end and the familiar comforting sound of the approaching Bradford station, he might have choked to death from the sheer weight of his own self-induced psychotic pressure: any benefit he'd gained in the convalescent home had been dashed in minutes in the Clayton tunnel. How he managed to pull himself together and walk off the train in such an exhausted and inebriated state beggars belief – but he'd managed it, and even managed to find his way home later that evening.

That night Berry had the most horrific nightmare. Grotesque apparitions and scores of faces twisted with the agony of eternal damnation lunged at his mind's eye – one, then another; then a dozen or more at a time: voices, screaming in agony with deafening condemnation overlaid with the hideous cackling of laughter – the pit of Hell was spewing its worst. His very soul felt the crushing weight of multiple sins: sins of the lives he'd taken; his own sins, the heaviest of all. He saw his house, wife and children. He was a failure as a husband, a failure as a father and a failure as a human being. Suddenly, like a black-out, all went quiet as if some single controlling phantom had ordered a hush and was demanding to speak. Berry was now looking at a barren volcanic landscape riddled with cracks and fissures from which spurted hissing jets of steam and smoke. His attention was drawn to a rising plume of swirling vapour; now centre stage in the vision. He felt as if he was sitting in an audience, a court room and was waiting for a judge to pass sentence.

"Guilty Berry! ... guilty as charged, beyond all reasonable doubt ... guilty!"

The condemnation of the whispering voice from the coiling mist was absolute. Berry tried to stop his ears but it was useless.

"Atone Berry ... atone ... a life for a life ... there's no other way ... it's the Great Law ... Atone!"

CHAPTER 15
THE TRAIN

The terrible night eventually gave way to dawn, and after his awful ordeal Berry now knew what he had to do.

Possessed with determination his mind was clear that there was now only one way out; one way out of this crushing mental and spiritual torture and this miserable life altogether. There was an express mail train due through Bradford from Newcastle later in the afternoon which would probably pass through the Queensbury and Clayton tunnels. Also another would be due out of Bradford to head up north about the same time. This meant that there would be a good chance that the two trains would pass in opposite direction in either one tunnel or the other. He would gather together bare minimum items; just enough to give the impression that he was going on another job so as to fool Sarah – who by now was past caring anyway.

Then he would buy a one way ticket to Halifax, find an empty compartment with an outside carriage door; at the right time open it, and fling himself out into the path of the passing express as they met in the tunnel. It would be quick, effective and all over and done with. And in his confused chaotic way he believed that he would have atoned for all those souls he had sent to oblivion.

Of course he had slept little during the night and had risen early to creep about the house during the early hours of the morning without disturbing the rest of the family. Sitting in the large armchair of his study he gazed round for the last time at the many pictures and artefacts he had collected over the years as souvenirs and reminders of his professional duties. Picking up pen and paper he then began scribbling a note, thinking at least he owed his family some kind of farewell and explaining that he saw no other way out and they would be better off without him. Finally, stuffing a half bottle of whisky into a small canvas satchel, plus his gloves and scarf to fill out its shape, he headed for the door. As he made way to the road outside he turned to glance at the home he was going to leave for the last time. Sarah was peering through the window; with a sad, yet compassionate, expression in her eyes as if she knew this would be the last time she would see him. Berry's heart was torn …

he couldn't hold the gaze any longer, and with a feeble hand gesture turned and went his way.

After he had ambled along for a short distance he decided to take a detour through the park on his way to the Midland station. It was still too early in the morning and the pubs wouldn't be open until much later, which of course would provide him with suitable anaesthetic for the deed he was about to commit. The train to Halifax was not due in until the afternoon, so he had time on his hands. In the meantime he would find a secluded spot near the edge of the park near some old derelict buildings away from view, and finalise his plans. Taking further inspiration and comfort from a nip or two of whisky, Berry snugged himself into a dusty corner of an old disused outbuilding; shrugged up his collar from the morning damp and settled into a dark depression.

"Wake up Berry Wake up!" Suddenly a harsh voice shook him back to reality. Had he been asleep for hours, not realising it?

Berry sharply looked around expecting to find someone who might have crept up on him during his slumber, but the place was empty.

"C'mon lad … it's time to go … y' know the routine."

It came again, this time as a whisper but with a quiet authority. Was there someone playing tricks? Or was he hearing this inside his head? It was familiar. He'd heard it before somewhere. Was it his own voice, and was it some kind of ghoulish dream raking up all the past times he'd escorted men to the gallows? Fumbling his pocket watch he squinted his eyes to focus on the time. It was past midday – he'd slept the entire morning and the Halifax train would be in soon. *Best get a move on,* he thought.

But no! ... What am I doing?... No!... I don't want this. I don't want to die ... I'm innocent ... innocent! Leave me alone – go away!

Downing the last of the whisky Berry stood to his feet flinging the empty bottle to one side in protest.

"Shut up Berry! Don't argue with us." It was if an iron cloak suddenly possessed him – he was no longer his own property. Behind the voices were real entities who were now in control and beginning to cajole and bully him on his way. This was physical. Feeling a distinct push between his shoulders he lunged forwards almost tripping over his own feet in the process. There was no way back now; he was committed. A timeless vacuum was sweeping him along with a pre-ordained destiny. Everything was under control; everything would be in its place with the clockwork of military precision. This was his day, his moment, and his execution.

"Aft'noon Mr Berry – goin' far today sir?"

Berry gave poor response to the cheerful ticket Officer who obviously knew him from the many journeys he'd taken in the past.

"Halifax – one way," was about all he got from him.

Fumbling in his pocket for the money Berry surprisingly found just the right change for the ticket enabling him to move on without having to engage in any further conversation.

There were a few moments spare as the train had not yet arrived in the station enabling the exhausted man to slump his penitent frame onto one of the platform benches, take his time and hopefully make some sense out of what he was supposed to be doing.

"Hello Sir… are you alright?" Startled by the appearance of what seemed to be a young man suddenly sitting at the side of him, Berry vacantly looked up from his crouched posture. He was a strange looking man with a Southern accent; old before his time with slightly greying hair as if life at some time had dealt him a bad hand, yet oddly familiar. The man had a kindness about him which

138

momentarily put Berry at ease, then in a gentle voice he continued:

"Excuse me sir for being rather blunt … but tell me … if you were to die tonight do you think you'd go to Heaven or Hell?"

Berry was totally taken aback by the sheer inappropriate nature of the question.

"What?"

"I meant to say sir, are you saved? And if you were to –"

"Have nothing to do with him!" interrupted an ear splitting voice inside him.

"Get away from him! … he's not one of us … don't listen!"

Berry felt as if his head was about to burst, and clawing his ears and shaking his head lunged to his feet.

"Leave me alone … leave me alone all of you!" he shrieked causing much attention on the platform.

 "Take your hands off me stop pulling me … get off !"

Convinced he was in some kind of tug o' war between the two powers Berry found himself spinning like a top much to further amusement of onlookers.

When he eventually stopped to face the stranger there was no one there – he'd gone!

"Ha - ha! … he didn't last long, did he Berry?" mocked a cackling voice.

"Look! ... the train – c'm on Berry best get a move on."

During the mystical encounter the train had arrived and was standing in the station with people beginning to board.

"Quick! Get on," came the voice again.

Suddenly, as if transported, Berry found himself sitting in an empty compartment with just the right privacy he needed for the job in hand. As the carriage door swiftly slammed behind him, thus sealing his destiny, the train pulled out of the station.

He didn't have to wait long. Just a few miles up the track came the first tunnel – the Clayton tunnel. This was it he thought – *best act now… get it over with.* But there seemed to be a new inner struggle now. Since his encounter with the stranger he was beginning to have second thoughts – a new reluctance to end his life – a fight was beginning to take shape.

"Get up Berry – get up!" The harsh voice drove him to his feet.

Berry stiffened with resistance, digging his heel in against the physical arrest of demonic guards forcing him towards the door, but it was useless they were too strong and his strength had all but gone.

"That's it … stand there … that's the spot … you know the routine," the voice went on.

"Open the window … open it now – quick, that's it … good lad."

In submissive obedience to his executioner Berry was now standing against the outside door of the compartment with the sliding window down, poking his head into the rushing cold air. Soon the hooded darkness of the tunnel would take away any last light he would ever see of this world, and he would be plunged into eternity.

CHAPTER 16

HONLY BELIEVE

Since his encounter with the mysterious stranger on the platform it was if Berry had been numbed into a dream-like state. Totally powerless and entirely at the mercy of supernatural forces that were driving him on, he had just about given up – "dead man walking" – he no longer cared, like many of the condemned men and women he too had once sent to their fate.

By now the whole tunnel, including his own compartment was filled with engine smoke; half choking and eyes streaming in the slipstream, he was becoming more and more desperate for an end to it all.

Get ready James. How seductive was that? *James ... James ...* how subtly personal – was this the whispering inner charm of his hideous companion? Was it Hell's final disarming tactic to seal his fate?

Look ... the light ... here it comes ... watch! Again the whisper.

An echoing wail of a steam whistle indicated the mail express had begun to enter the far end of the tunnel and was approaching rapidly. With large quantities of smoke and steam belching from her stack, and a bright headlight piercing the darkness, she was thundering in full tilt, scheduled to pass straight through Bradford without stopping in order to meet Southern deadlines.

Berry stiffened again with fear – sweat and vapour pouring and rising from him. He became suddenly aware of the sheer gravity of the decision he was about to make. He could see glowing red-hot coals and ash spewing from under the locomotive's firebox, between steaming pistons and the slicing steel wheels of its rolling undercarriage … his roaring, fiery chariot to Gehenna was almost here.

It's alright James … look to the light … leap into the light … only believe!

He hated darkness more than anything, and with the growing envelopment of a smoke filled compartment the idea of a soothing light was a better option to sway his decision. He pushed open the carriage door and stepping onto the metal sill of the doorway was poised to spring.

"Down there Berry – down!" A harsh voice had stepped in to overrule.

"Aim for the fire – not the light – the fire – the wheels … go on – now!"

But it didn't matter either way; by now he'd given up. Flinging himself high into the air towards the obliterating light which was growing brighter by the second; semi-propelled by some unseen hand and with the sound of a cackling chorus cheering him on – it was all over!

The whole scene had now disappeared, and with it the train, the tunnel and time itself. But he was still conscious… still alive, in a twilight zone between illusion and reality; darkness and light, chaos and tranquillity; the eye of a storm which could erupt at any moment.

In his hyper conscious state he became aware of surrounding figures – countless faces he had once hooded and noosed from daylight, now grotesque in form, eagerly leering and clawing at him to claim possession. He fought and fought – kicking and thrashing about – had he arms and legs? He didn't know – desperate … so desperate!

Only believe … lad … only believe, came that soft whisper again, but this time he recognised it as someone fighting for him. He was aware that someone else was fighting his corner as well; there was a contest of principalities going on here, and the prize? – his very soul!

With a final burst of any last grain of faith he'd ever had in his life, Berry – the hangman screamed out for all he was worth:

"God have mercy on me! … J' Jesus help me … help me … please!"

Suddenly there was a loud "crack!" like the snapping of iron shackles or the bursting of a bronze door – something had finally yielded into retreat – gone! … leaving a momentary silence.

Berry felt he'd been alone for a while when gradually a new scene began to take form; again mysterious figures were peering down at him but this time they no longer had grotesque faces, but kind ones and were surrounded by myriads of angelic beings bathed in light.

"Only believe … Honly believe … James."

Berry felt a giggle coming on; then a chuckle. He'd heard this before – the plumber at the chapel in Exeter – that was it! Last time he was angry and ridiculed him; now he was amused – he loved him. He found himself laughing. He'd never done this for years – was it a dream?

But where am I? he thought.

"Open your eyes James … look up," came the same voice.

It's him! It's that … d'damn … p… lumber … it's old Wiggy!

James gingerly opened his eyes like a once blind man seeing for the first time. The kind faces he saw in his mind were now real, some of whom he was beginning to recognise from his own locality. Somewhere he was lying flat of his back, on the floor, looking up and gazing at a host of kind folk happily rejoicing to see him. And then a central figure with a smile so kind and warm – Smith Wigglesworth – the plumber!

James Berry was now laughing and laughing heartly – "Honly … hee - hee … h, honly… ha-hah!… honly believe he said."

By now he had the whole group of people euphorically laughing. Wigglesworth rocking to and fro on his heels fully aware the joke was on him but loving every moment; tears of joy streaming down his beautiful radiant face.

"B'but … w' where am I?" he said, giving everyone further reason to chuckle.

"Where! … where?" chuckled Wigglesworth.

"Why ... you're at Bowland Street Mission, flat on yer back, in the presence of the Lord ... hallelujah! ... ha-hah!"

How it had all worked out is a mystery, but somehow whether through some time portal, a twist of fate or just a sheer miracle, the horrific events on the train and tunnel had failed to download their cursed plan onto the matrix of his life.

"Whom the Son sets free is free indeed!" boomed the plumber.

"Arise James ... get up and walk in the name of Jesus!"

Pulling him by the hand Wigglesworth helped him to his feet. Feeling strength in his limbs he sprang up in response, jumping and leaping like the miraculously healed lame man in the Bible.

He was free! Jumping, dancing and laughing feeling light as a feather, like a baby; tears of joy, re-born ... saved ... saved from a life of misery and saved from eternal damnation; the hangman had cheated the executioner, and the powers of darkness were well and truly shaken!

It took quite a time for Berry to gather himself after his rapturous encounter, eventually being ushered to sit somewhere more comfortable.

"C'mon laddie, let's get thee a cup o' tea shall we … tha looks as if tha needs it. Tha's 'ad a bit of an ordeal tha knows – we'll 'ave a chat," said Smith in his broad Yorkshire dialect.

Sitting to one side the small gathering listened intently whilst Smith began unfolding some of the answers to James's questions.

"Tell me Mr Wigglesworth … what's happened? I'm sure I was on that train, I'm sure I jumped into the path of that express – I should be dead! – facing justice I deserve."

Beaming a cheerful smile and peering up over his spectacles from his small Bible he'd been flipping through, Smith began to explain:

"Well my friend, it's known as the Great Exchange. When Christ died on that cross at Calvary he took all the sins of the world on his shoulders – all the vilest of wickedness that mankind could ever commit – He bore it all. In other words James He took all yours – He took your place, exchanging your judgement for his. The Bible tells us we've all fallen short of the glory of God; we all deserve punishment of one sort or another. But we are saved by the atoning sacrifice of Jesus – his blood shed for you and me on that cross – that's GRACE! All we have to do is acknowledge our needs and shortcomings – repent and accept the gift … honly … ha-ha … *I know* … ONLY believe! Simple as that – it's a gift – just as you did just now. The Great Exchange! Christ's atoning sacrifice on the cross. What the Great Law couldn't do, Jesus did! He came to earth to do a job that we could not complete ourselves. Grace, James, through faith – GRACE! What happened to you on the train … I don't know. But what I do know is; that the devil had a scheme for your life, and it would have happened except for a miracle, and through that you're here today – somebody at some time in the past must have been praying for you."

To use the term *tea and sympathy* would be an understatement to say the least; yet cups of tea and conversation went on well into the evening. James had never known such love from just a few simple folk – tearfully overwhelmed. The evening finally rounded off with a suggestion from Smith's wife Polly:

"About your wife James – about Sarah … do you think she might wonder where you are … shall we go now and tell her the good news?"

"Aye lass … aye, I think we will an' all … I'll say a big amen to that!"

Wiping his eyes and taking a deep intake of breath, James boldly rose to his feet with a new confidence, much encouraged by hearty cheers and applause from the fellowship.

"C'mon then folks, now's the time – let's go!" said James taking Smith and Polly by the arm.

Standing near the outer door was the young man who had first spoken to James at the station. Up until now he'd kept in the background and remained unnoticed during the excitement. On seeing James he reached to shake his hand.

"Thank you my friend, thank you for everything you did for me on that platform – I owe you my life!" said James clasping the man's hand with both of his.

The two stared intently at each other for a few seconds; there was a bond, a connection blurred by the shifting of time; it was beyond explanation but real enough to fill James with gratitude.

"Arr … yore welcome me friend … God bless ye!"

Again that Southern voice was comfortably familiar. James gave him a last curious glancing nod and walked out into the street.

Outside the world looked different; new, clean and sharp in colourful contrast. James felt as if he'd embraced the world for the first time – indeed he was, a new man.

Rounding the corner of Cliffe Road he stopped to gather his thoughts.

"Let me go ahead Smith; you can follow in a couple of minutes. I'd just like a moment with Sarah alone, and then we can tell her the story."

On opening the door James walked in; stood in the hall entrance and shouted:

"Sarah! … Sarah! … are you there?"

"Hello – hello … is that y'you James?"

"It is Sarah my love … it is indeed … I'm home Sarah – I'm home!"

EPILOGUE

Artistic license gives writers the opportunity to take a rest from the rigid format of keeping to a factual script of history and allows their minds the freedom to wonder off into the enriched, colourful lanes and byways of creative imagination; painting pictures on the reader's mind, and drawing them into the very page.

Although the writer of this short historical novella has taken the liberty to depart from the facts in order to give the ebb and flow of creative effect, it has to be said that much of what has been written is based on true and documented accounts which took place in the lives of at least four of the persons mentioned in this story:-

<u>John "Babbacombe" Lee</u>: Accused of the murder of Miss Emma Anne Keyes did indeed defy the gallows three times on the 23rd February 1885, and James Berry was the hangman. Lee was subsequently given penal servitude, but what happened to him on his eventual release from prison is uncertain.

<u>Miss Emma Anne Keyes</u>: A highly respected lady who lived in Babbacombe, was the tragic victim of a brutal act of murder on November 15th 1884. To this day the real perpetrator was never brought to justice, although strong suspicions were later aimed towards the lawyer – Reginald Gwynne Templar – who, it was claimed; "died shortly after through insanity".

<u>James Berry</u>: A notorious 19th century hangman, and one of the first to devotedly carry out the "humane" methods of execution developed by William Marwood. Berry struggled with the whole concept of the death sentence throughout his career as a hangman, which eventually had untold effect on his health. After his conversion under the ministry of Smith Wigglesworth he became one of the early campaigners for the abolition of capital punishment, and an evangelical preacher of the gospel up until his death in 1913.

<u>Smith Wigglesworth</u>: An outstanding apostle of the Christian faith; a plumber from Bradford who travelled the world preaching the Gospel of Jesus, and was one of the early pioneers of what is known today as the Renewal Movement throughout the Christian church world-wide. History records many accounts of astounding miracles – including raising the dead! But as Smith would probably agree; the greatest miracle is to see a changed life, and it has been the purpose of my story to simply show this. I would like to conclude by adding Smith's own testimony of an event which took place one evening in 1902, given in a sermon which was later published in his book, *Faith that Prevails* (1938). Quote:-

There was a notable character in the town in which I lived who was known as the worst man in the town. He was so vile, and his language was so horrible, that even wicked men could not stand it. In England they have what is known as the public hangman who has to perform all the executions. This man held that appointment and he told me later that he believed that when he performed the execution of men who had committed murder, the demon power that was in them would come upon him and that in consequence he was possessed with a legion of demons. His life was so miserable that he purposed to make an end of life. He went down to a certain depot and purchased a ticket. The English trains are much different from the

American. In every coach there are a number of small compartments and it is easy for anyone who wants to commit suicide to open the door of his compartment and throw himself out of the train. This man purposed to throw himself out of the train in a certain tunnel just as the train coming from an opposite direction would be about to dash past and he thought this would be a quick end to his life.

There was a young man at the depot that night who had been saved the night before. He was all on fire to get others saved and purposed in his heart that every day of his life he would get someone saved. He saw this dejected hangman and began to speak to him about his soul. He brought him down to our mission and there he came under a mighty conviction of sin. For two and a half hours he was literally sweating under conviction and you could see a vapour rising up from him. At the end of two and a half hours he was graciously saved. I said, "Lord, tell me what to do." The Lord said, "Don't leave him, go home with him." I went to his house.

When he saw his wife he said, "God has saved me." The wife broke down and she too was graciously saved. There was such a difference in that home. Even the cat knew the difference. There were two sons in that house and one of them said to his mother, "Mother, what is up in our house? It was never like this before. It is so peaceful. What is it?" She told him; "Father has been saved".

"The grace of God is sufficient for the vilest and He can take the most wicked of men and make them monuments of his grace. He did this with Saul of Tarsus at the very time he was breathing out threatenings and slaughter against the disciples of the Lord. He did it with James Berry the hangman. He will do it for hundreds more in response to our cries."

Smith Wigglesworth.

Also written by the author:

Facing the Stargate

Exploring the dimension of faith

By R H Brassington

Raised from the dead with a message from Jesus – still relevant for today!

The author uses a local event which took place in Chesterfield, Derbyshire, England in 1910 – making it of local interest to Derbyshire folk. It's a story about a man called William Sanderson who was miraculously raised from the dead and consequently cured of his life threatening illness. This particular account becomes a catalyst for thought, and acts as a driving theme throughout the book as the author investigates the *dimension of faith*.

Based on his own experience gleaned from debate and banter whether in the classroom workplace or pub, the author draws comparison with how the topical discussion almost always follows the same line of questions whenever someone sparks off the God debate. Evolution v Creation are hot on the agenda including Stephen Hawking's idea of a big bang from nothing.

Facing the Star-gate engages Christian apologetics by taking a holistic approach to science and the Bible. It is written simply by an ordinary man for ordinary folk who may be desperately trying to make sense of Christianity in today's fast changing and confusing world - or just simply to grab faith and get on with it! The book, uncompromising on the fundamental teaching on the bible's message of redemption, pulls no punches and makes no apologies when taking on the big guys in the science arena. Prepared to defend simply with biblical truth and the yard-stick of common sense the author quickly challenges the reader on those first order question -"Where have we come from, why are we here and where are we going"?

Finally as the overall question of our place in the universe cannot be ignored, the author takes us to what he believes is the pinnacle of human completion which man is created to achieve whilst in this present world – his final chapter: *Grace the final frontier* examines this important point.

Available from: Amazon.com, CreateSpace.com, Kindle and through other retail outlets.

Made in the USA
Columbia, SC
15 June 2019